THUNDER AND CLUCK

Smart vs. Strong

For Leo & Hallie
—J. E.

For every teacher—T. REX HUGS!
—M. T.

SIMON SPOTLIGHT
An imprint of Simon & Schuster Children's Publishing Division
1230 Avenue of the Americas, New York, New York 10020
This Simon Spotlight edition December 2021
Text copyright © 2021 by Jill Esbaum
Illustrations copyright © 2021 by Christopher M. Thompson
Manufactured in the United States of America 1021 LAK
10 9 8 7 6 5 4 3 2 1
This book has been cataloged with the Library of Congress.
ISBN 9781534486584 (hc)
ISBN 9781534486577 (pbk)
ISBN 9781534486591 (ebook)

THUNDER AND CLUCK

Smart vs. Strong

Written by **JILL ESBAUM**
Illustrated by **MILES THOMPSON**

Ready-to-Read *GRAPHICS*

Simon Spotlight
New York   London   Toronto   Sydney   New Delhi

HOW TO READ THIS BOOK

THUNDER and CLUCK are here to give you some tips on reading this book.

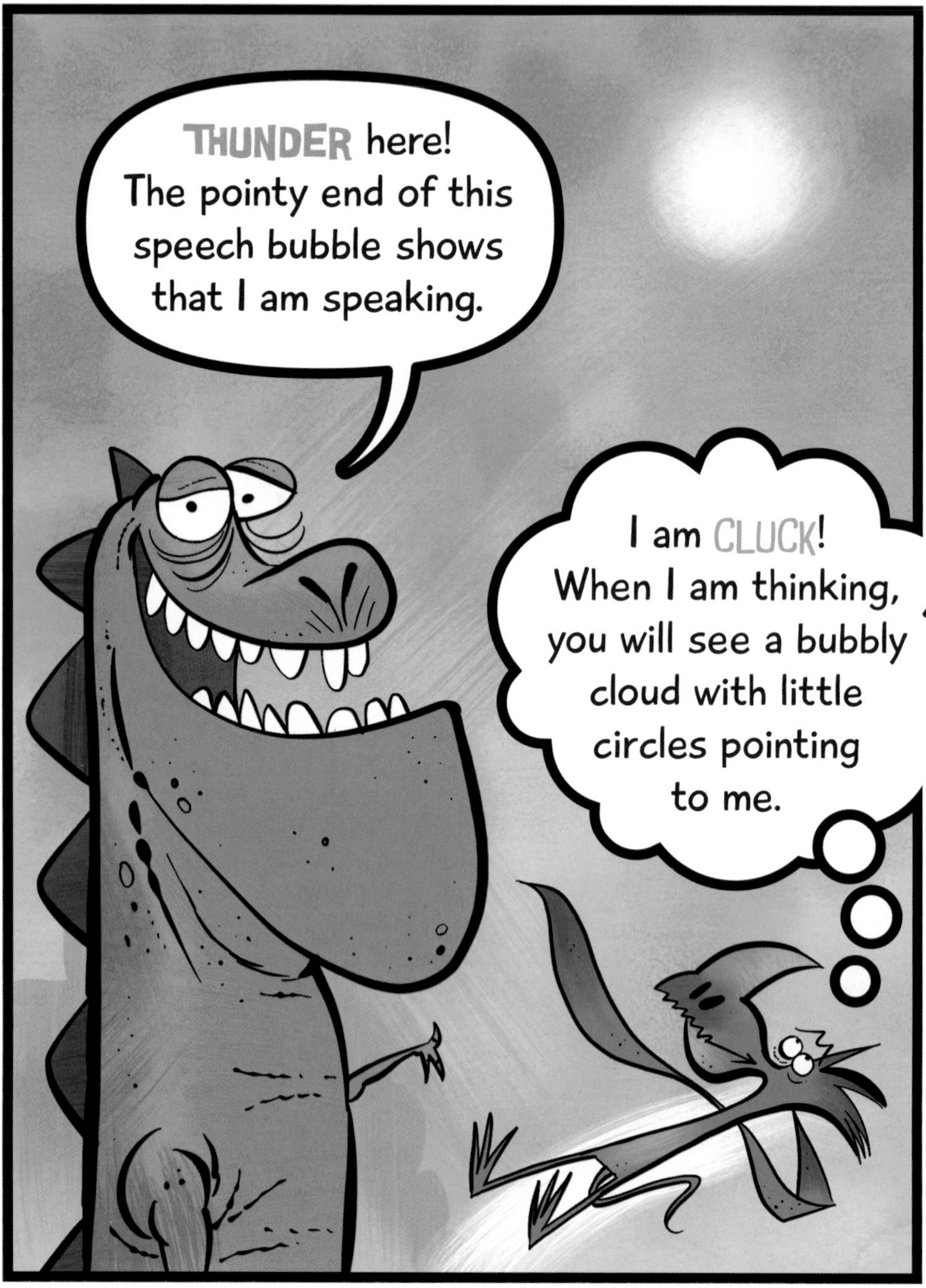
THUNDER here! The pointy end of this speech bubble shows that I am speaking.
I am CLUCK! When I am thinking, you will see a bubbly cloud with little circles pointing to me.

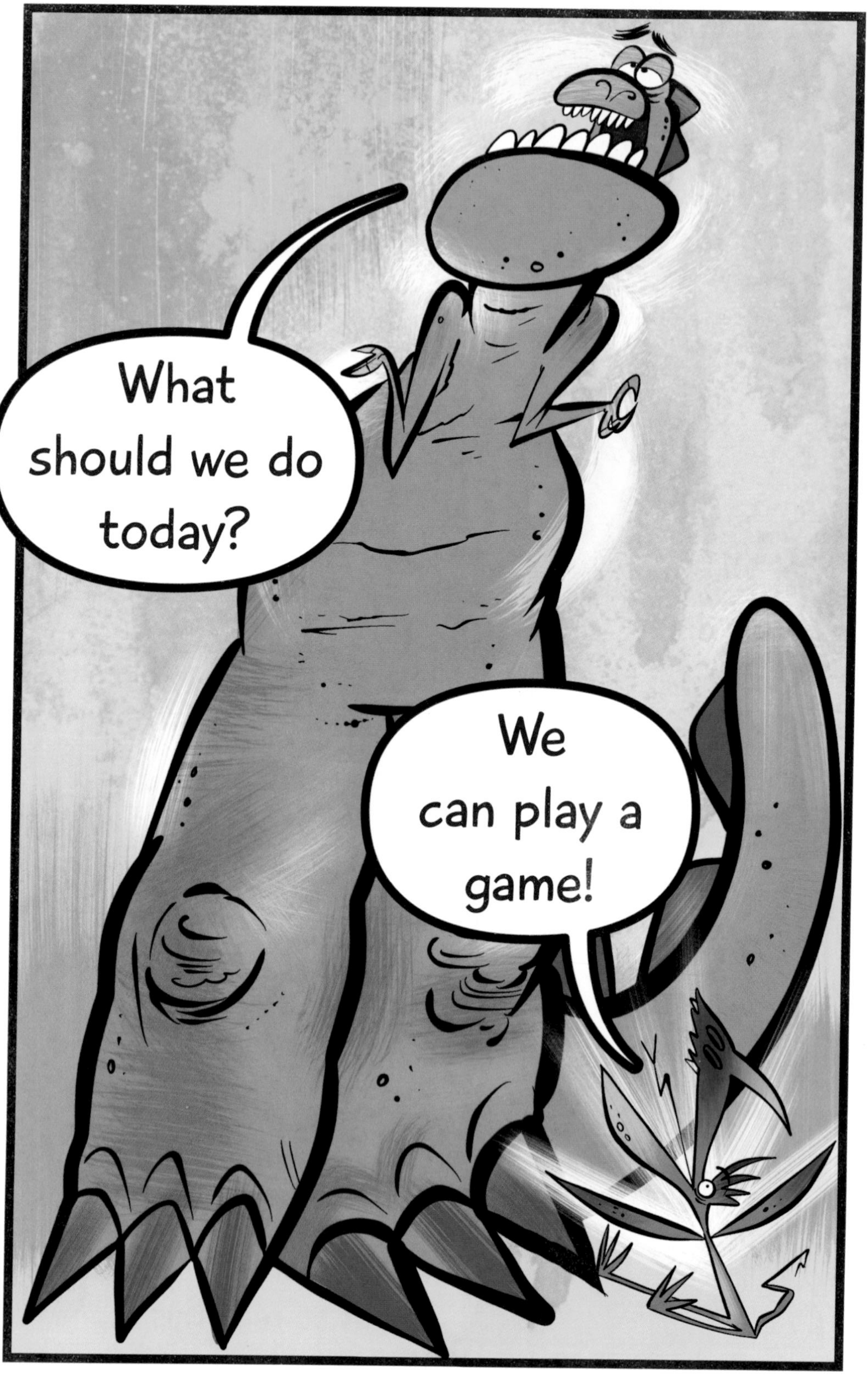
What should we do today?
We can play a game!

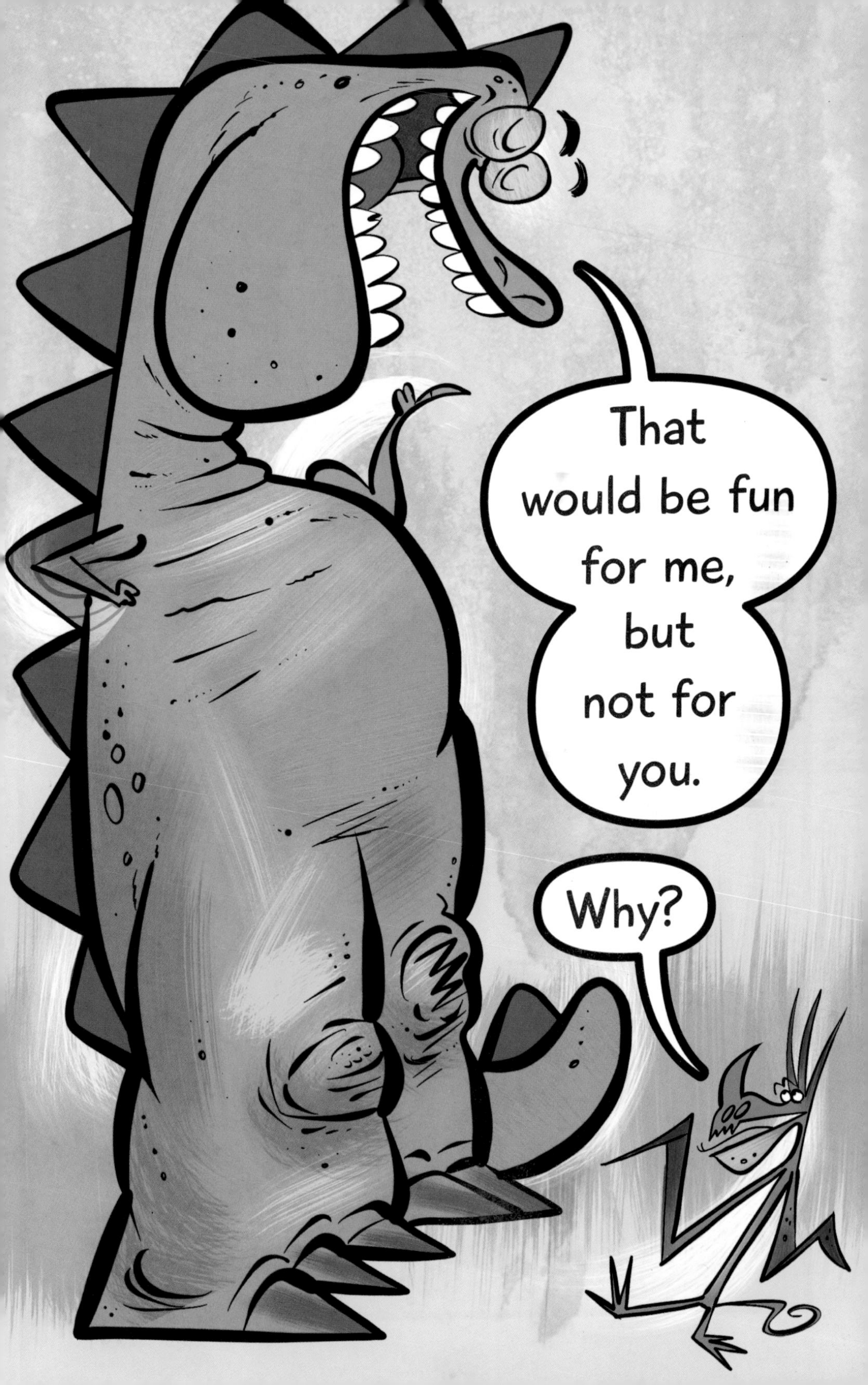
That would be fun for me, but not for you.
Why?

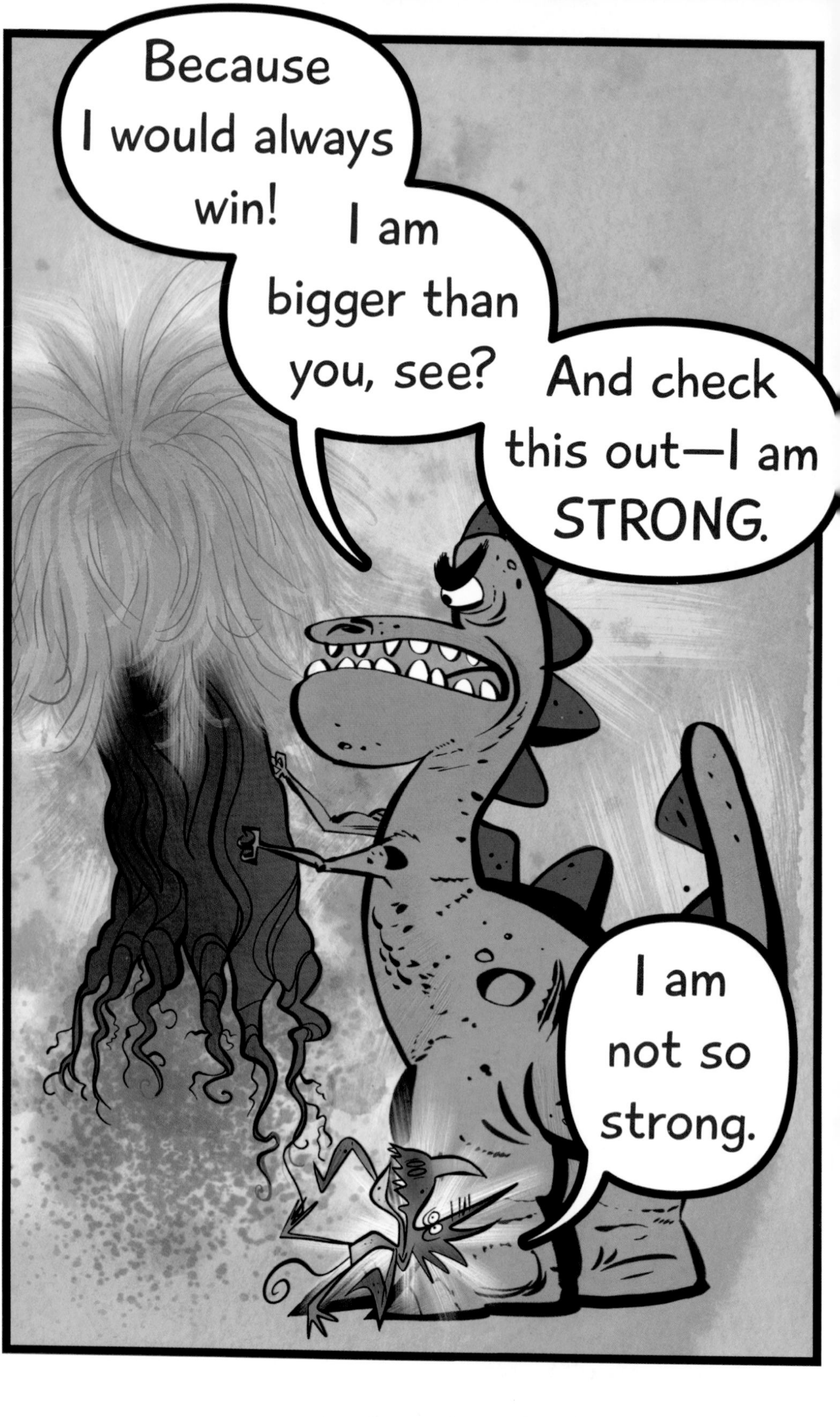
Because I would always win!
I am bigger than you, see?
And check this out—I am STRONG.
I am not so strong.

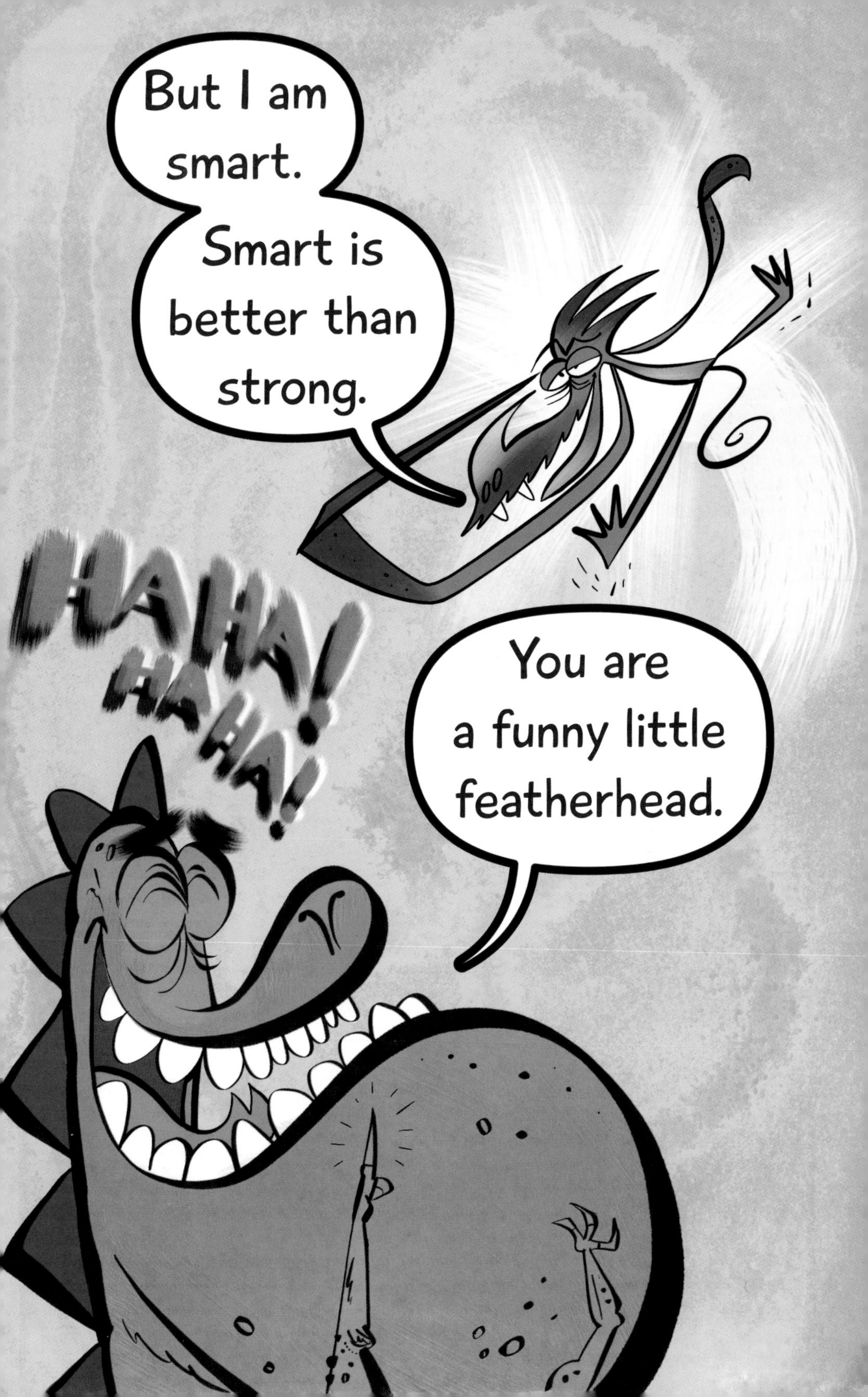
But I am smart.
Smart is better than strong.
HAHA! HA HA! HA!
You are a funny little featherhead.

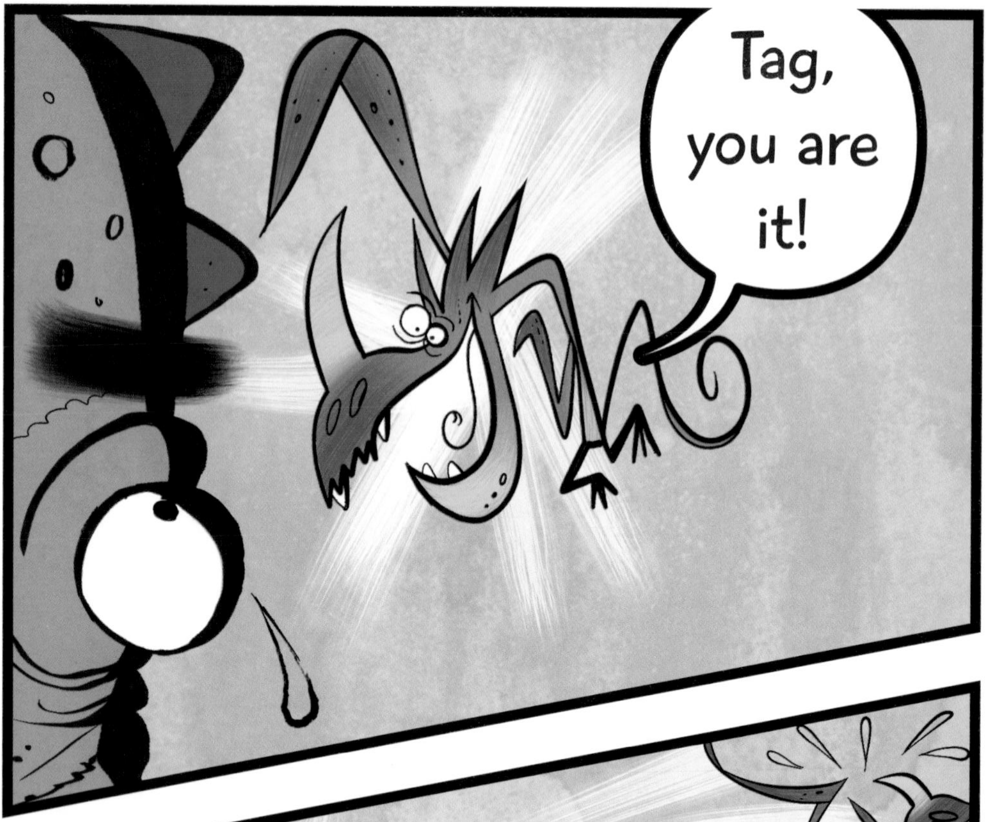
Tag, you are it!

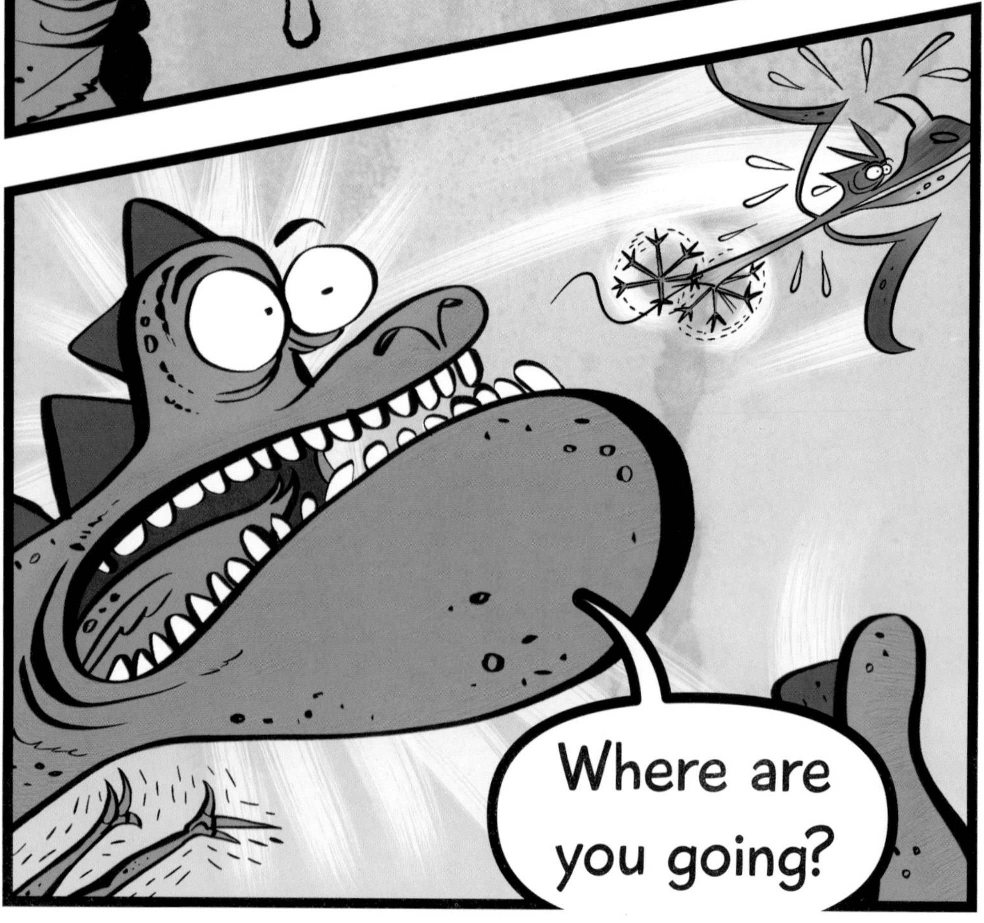
Where are you going?

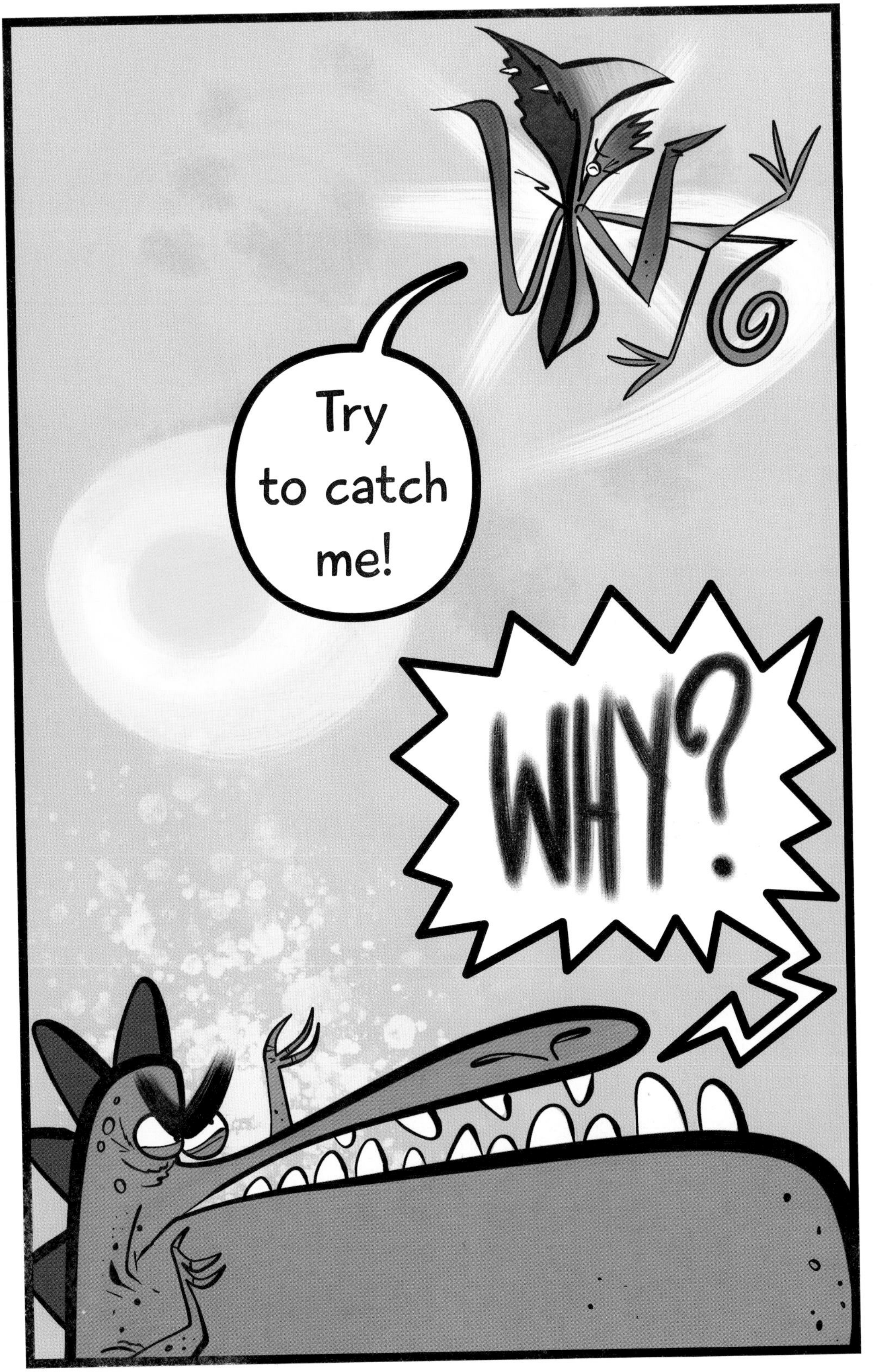
Try to catch me!
WHY?

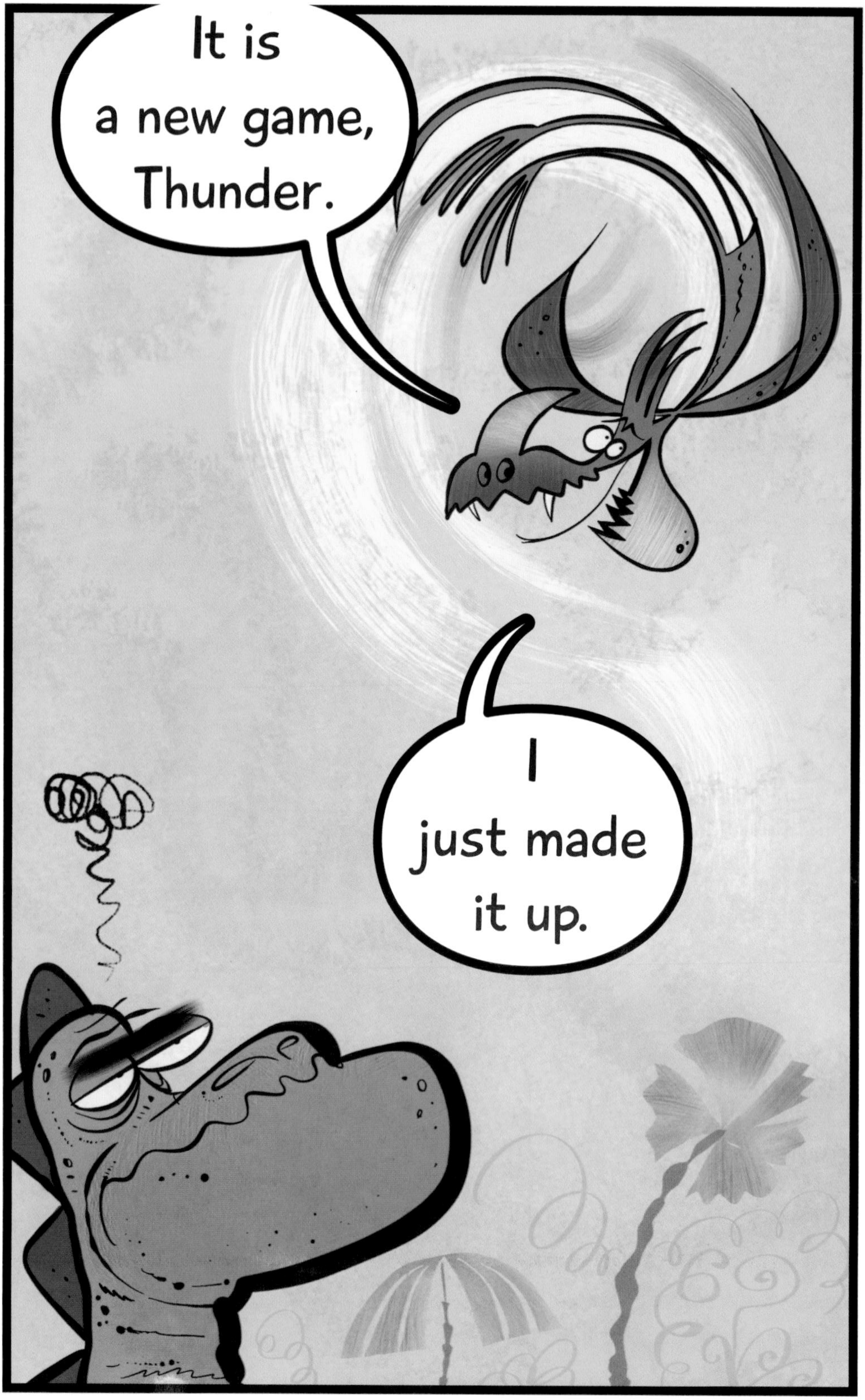
It is a new game, Thunder.
I just made it up.

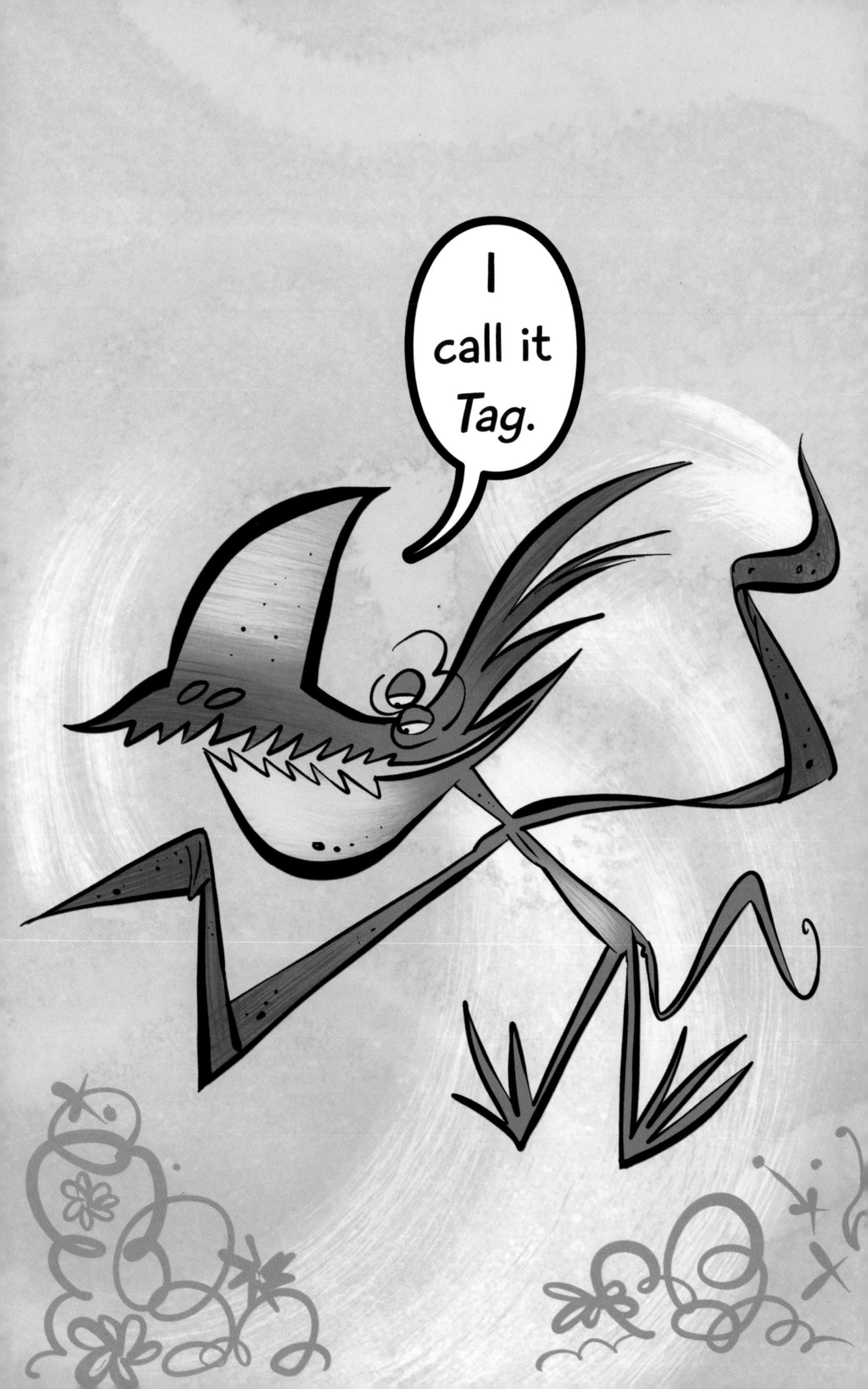
I call it *Tag.*

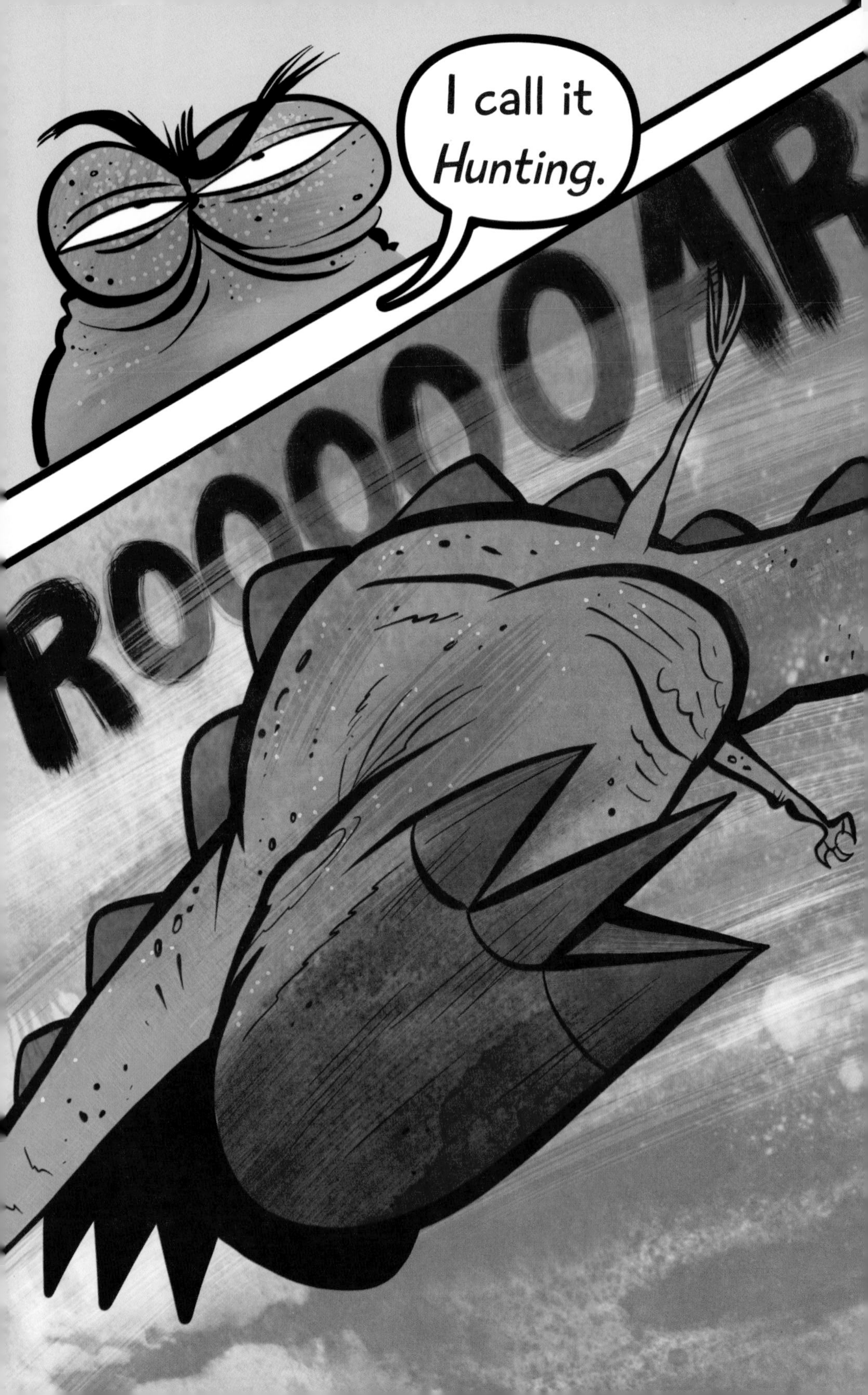
I call it *Hunting.*

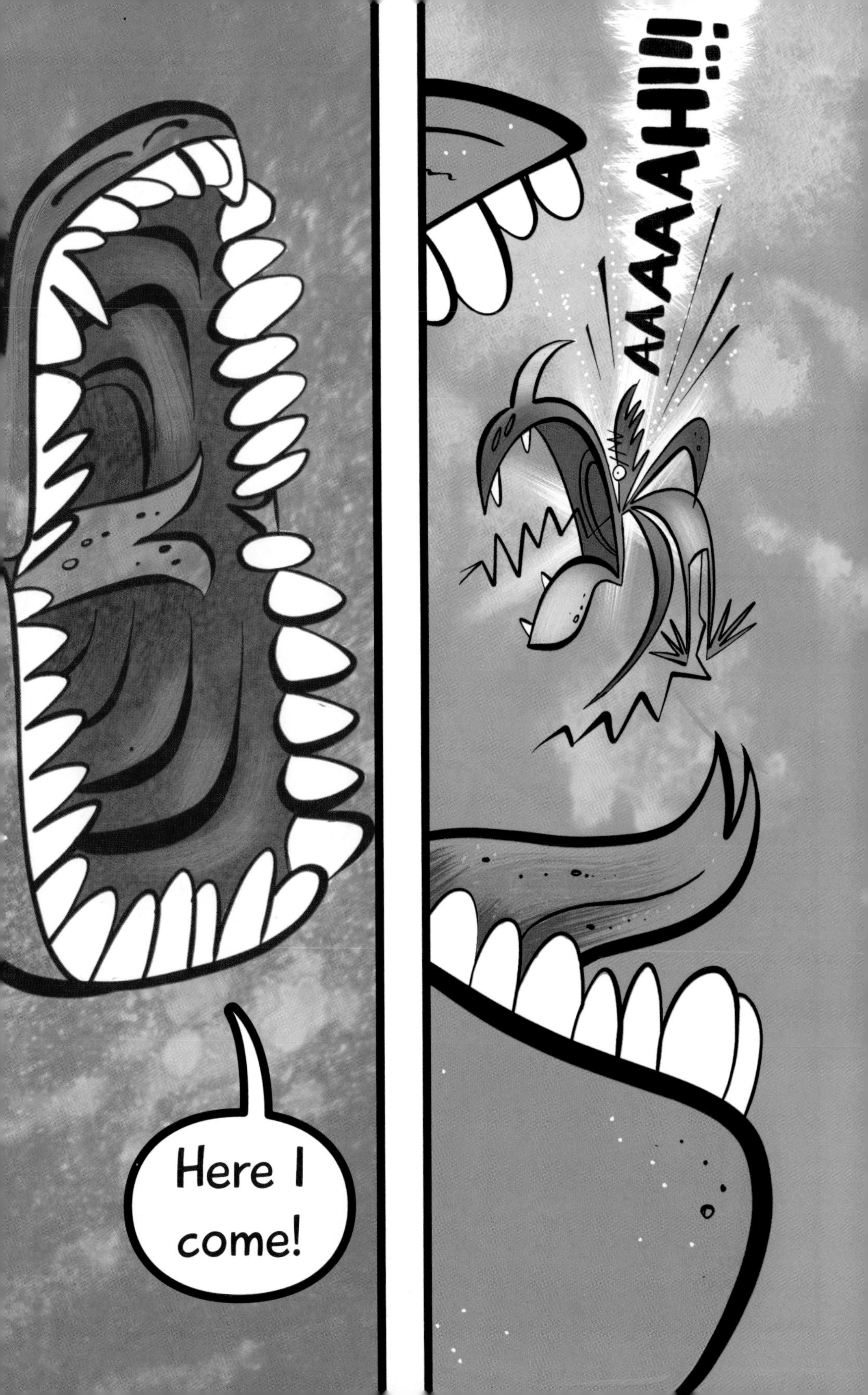
Here I come!
AAAAH!!!

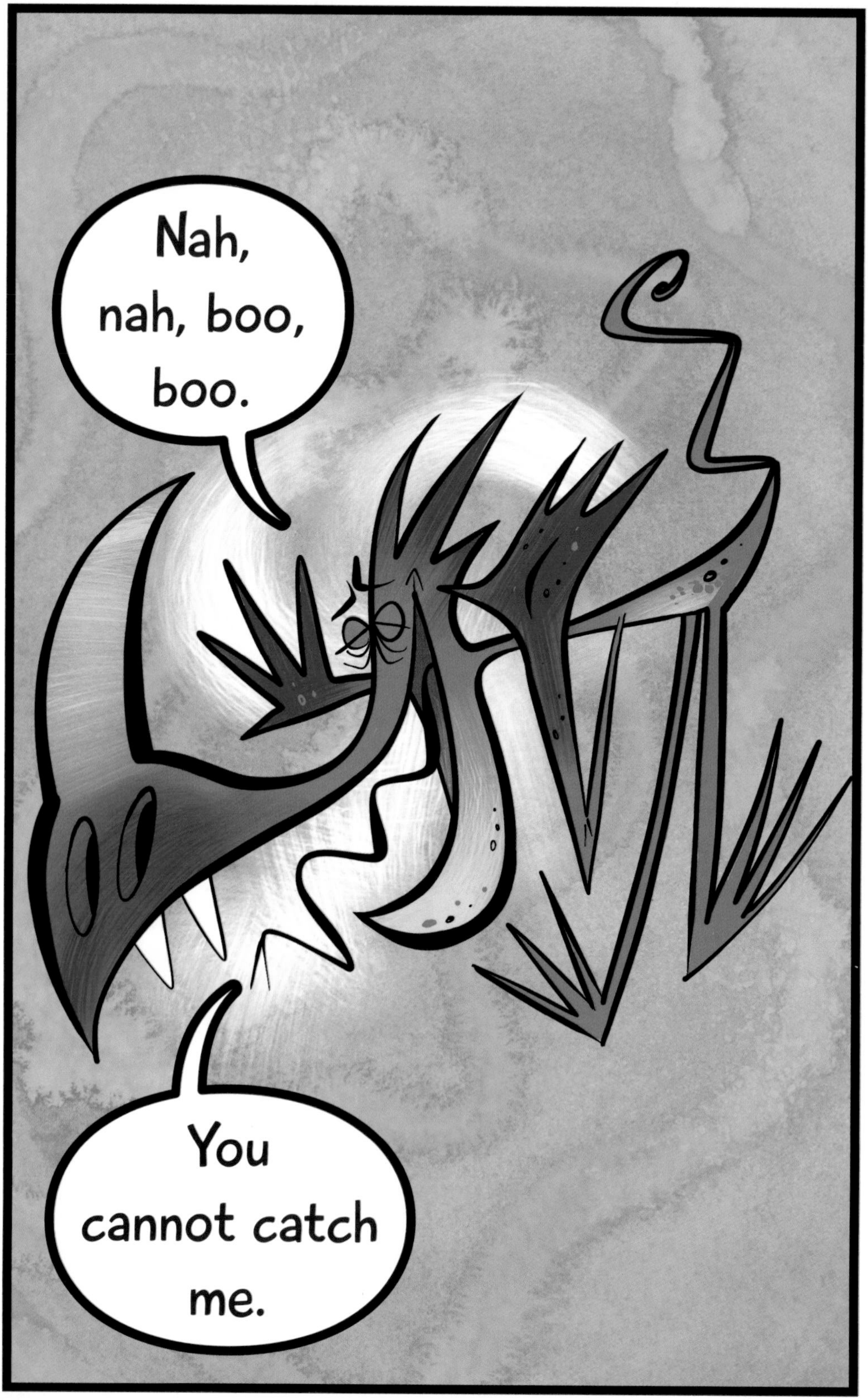
Nah, nah, boo, boo.
You cannot catch me.

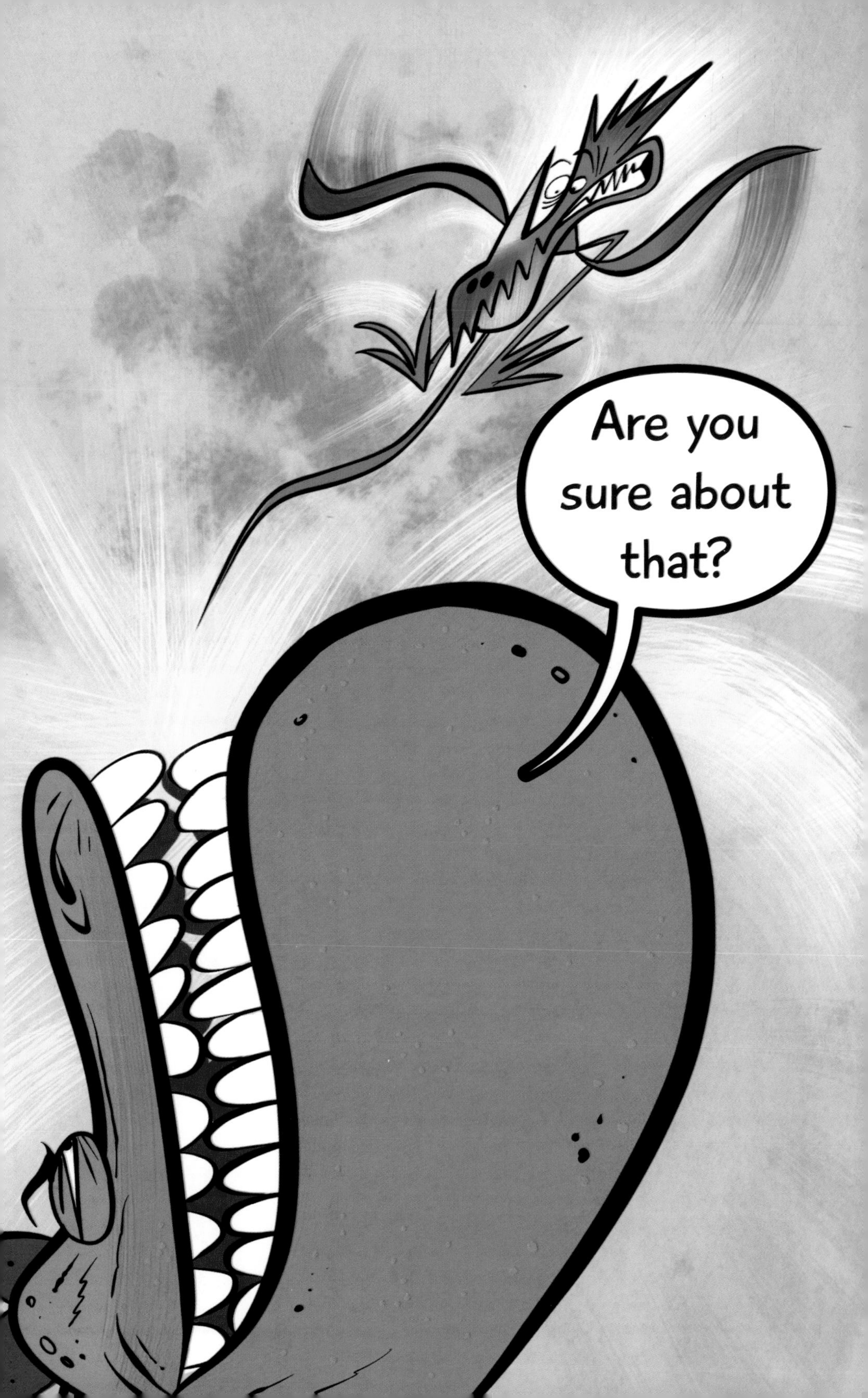
Are you sure about that?

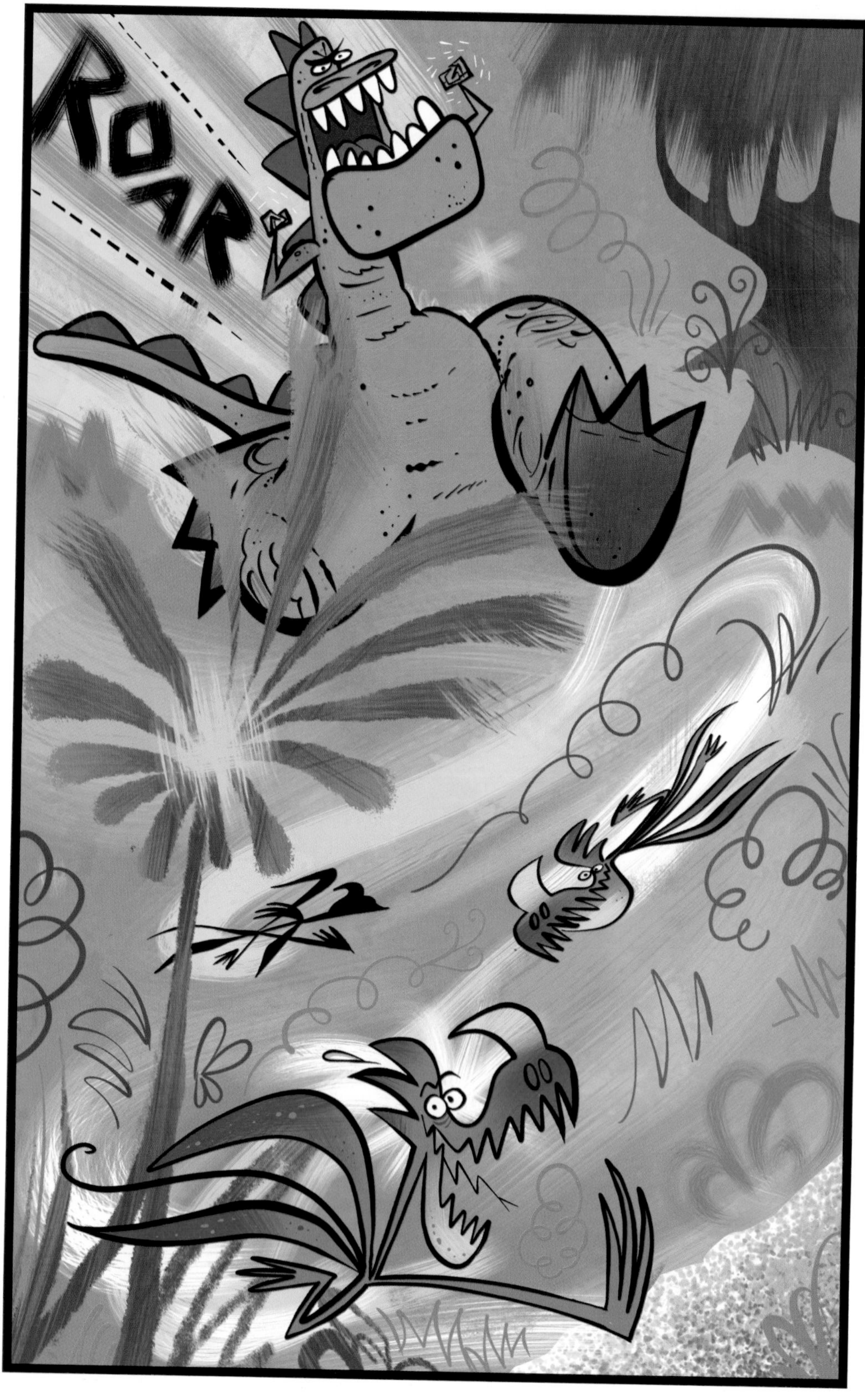
ROAR

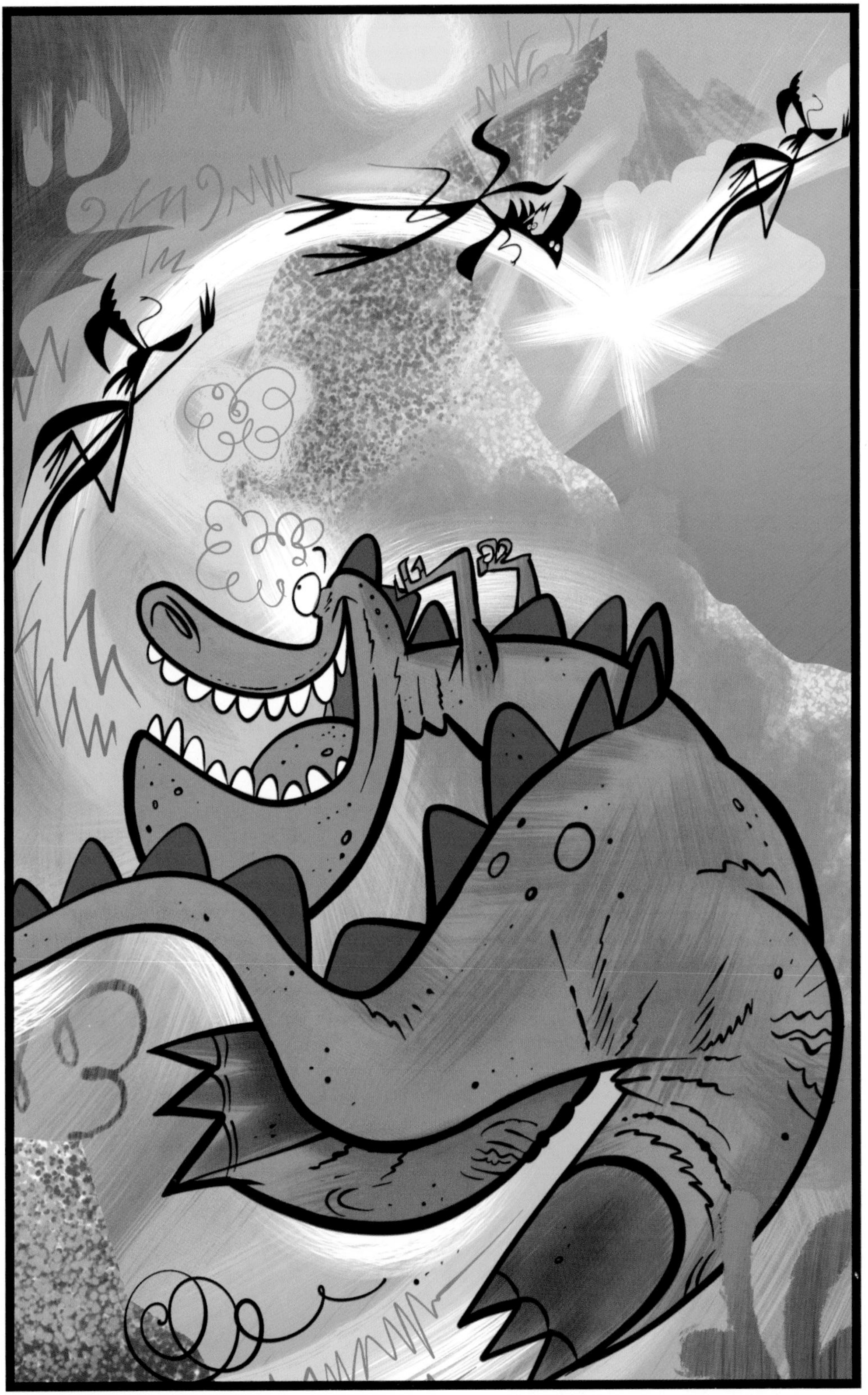

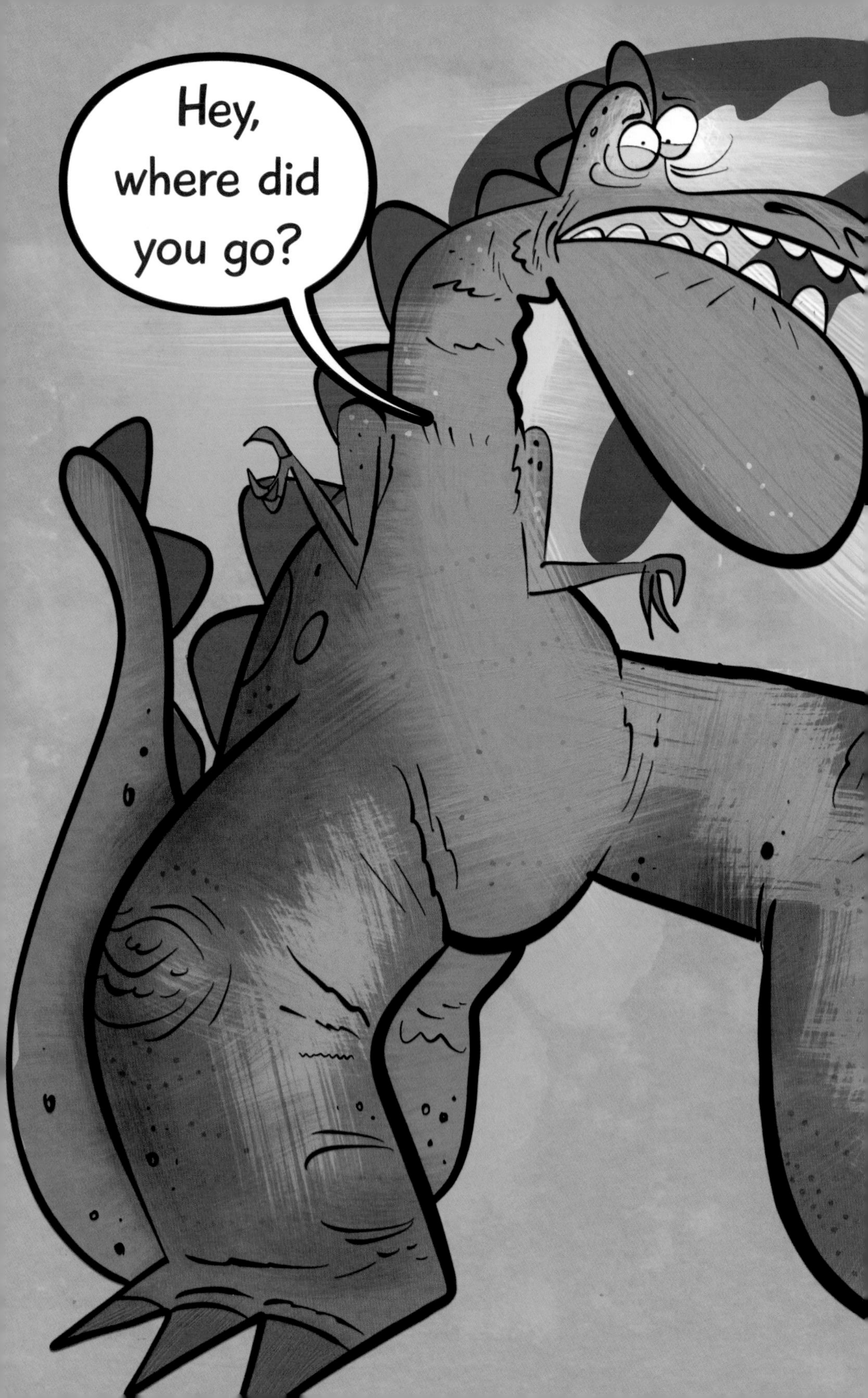
Hey, where did you go?

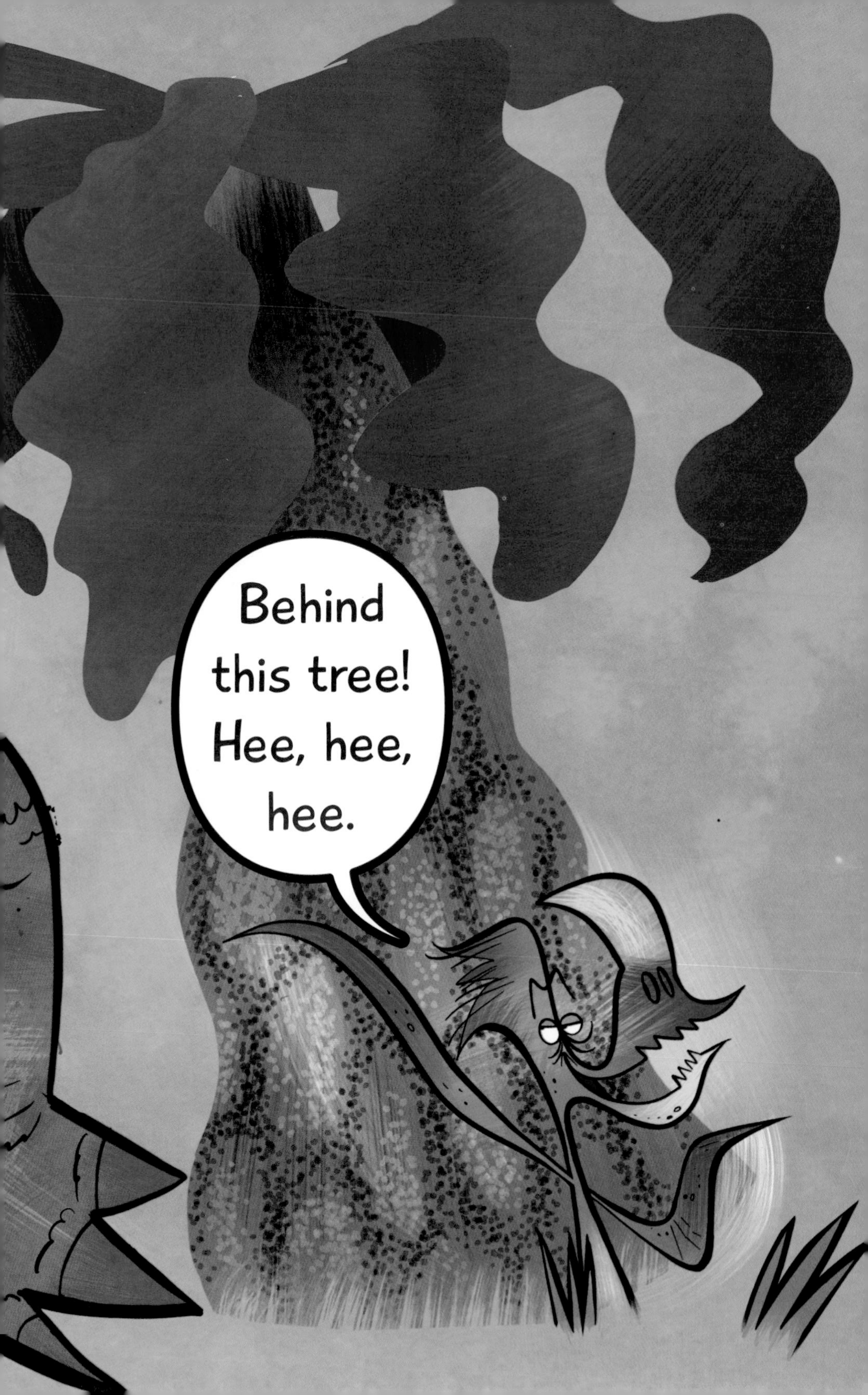
Behind this tree! Hee, hee, hee.

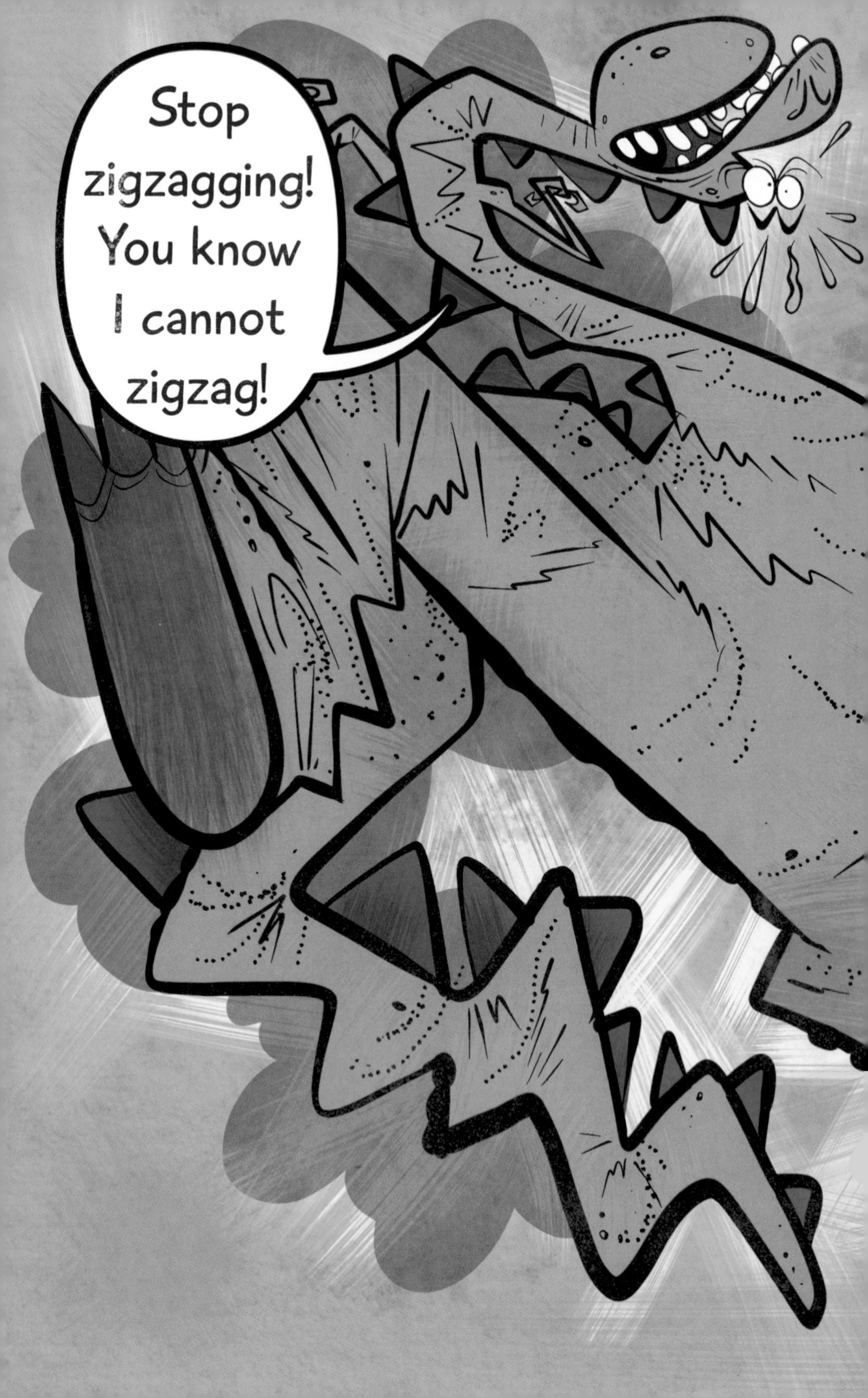
Stop zigzagging! You know I cannot zigzag!

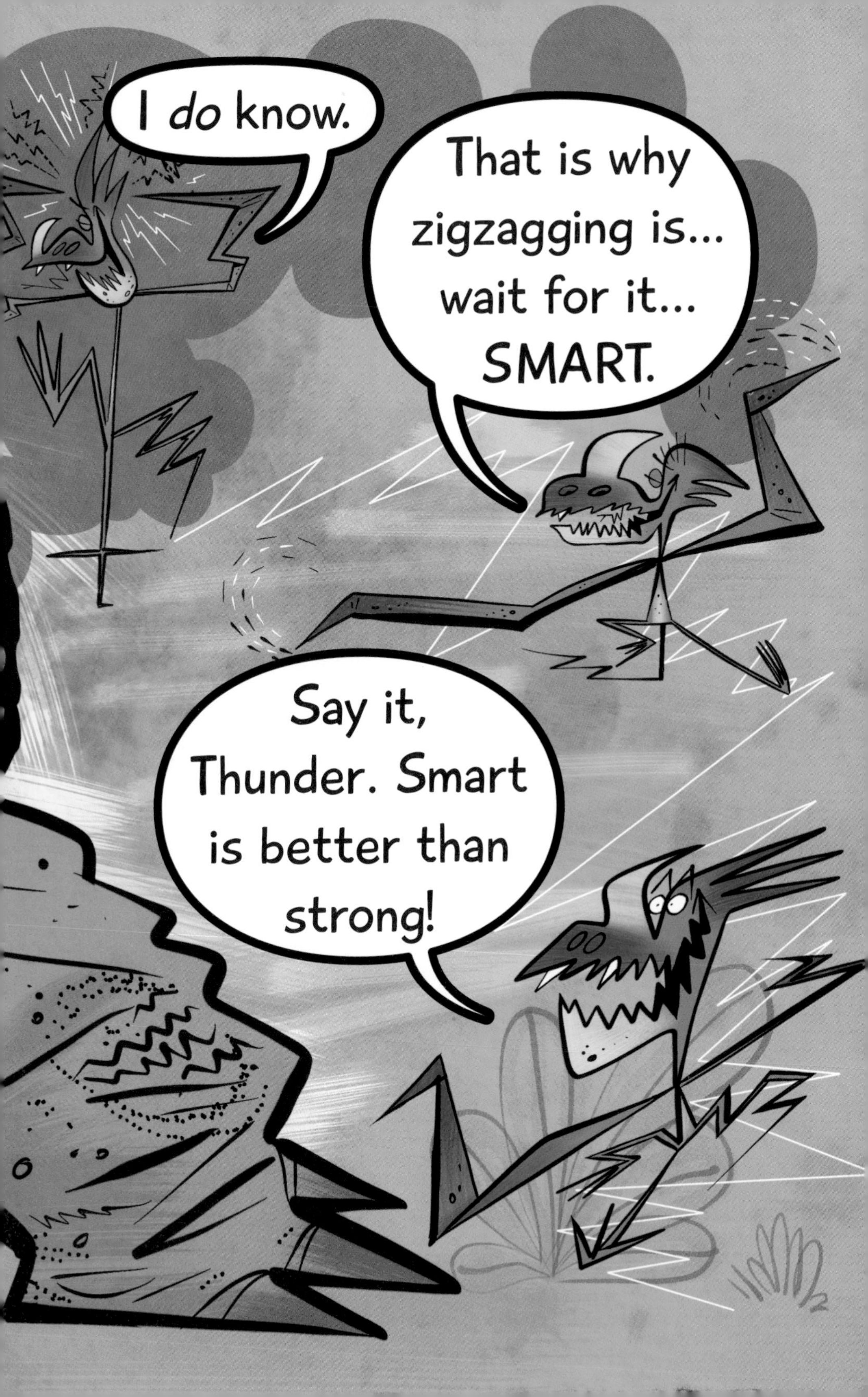

I *do* know.
That is why zigzagging is... wait for it... SMART.
Say it, Thunder. Smart is better than strong!

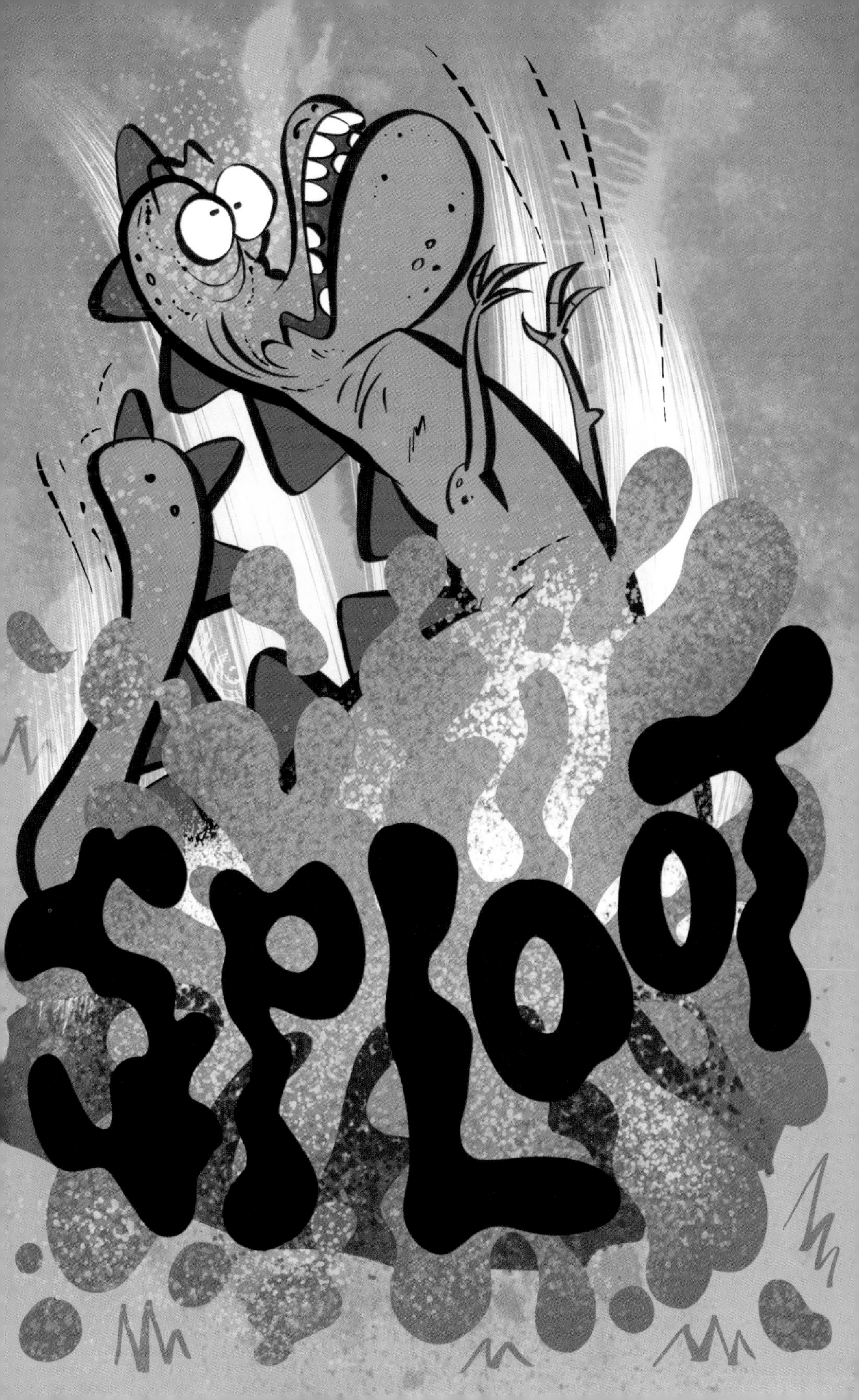
SPLOOT

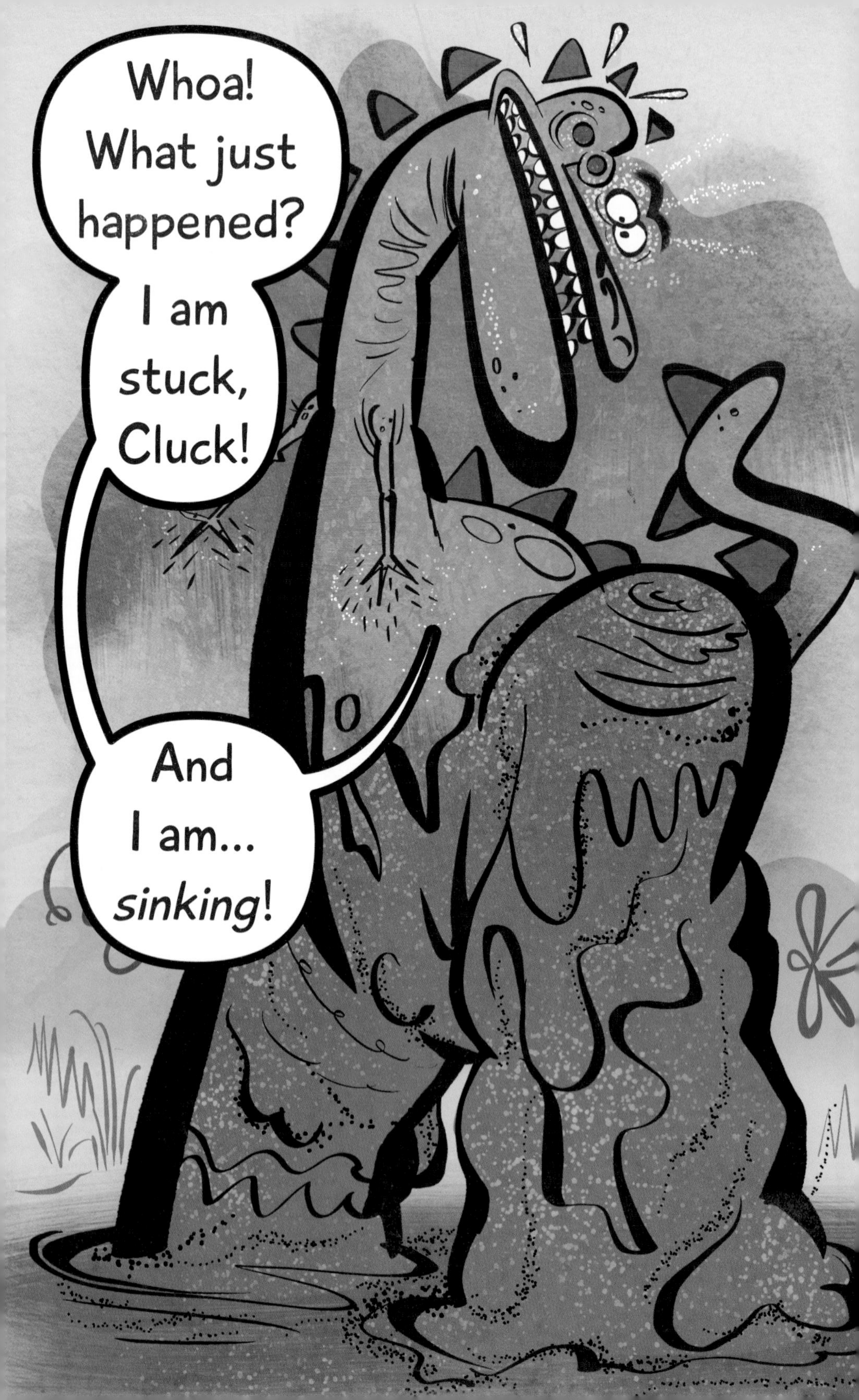
Whoa! What just happened?
I am stuck, Cluck!
And I am... *sinking*!

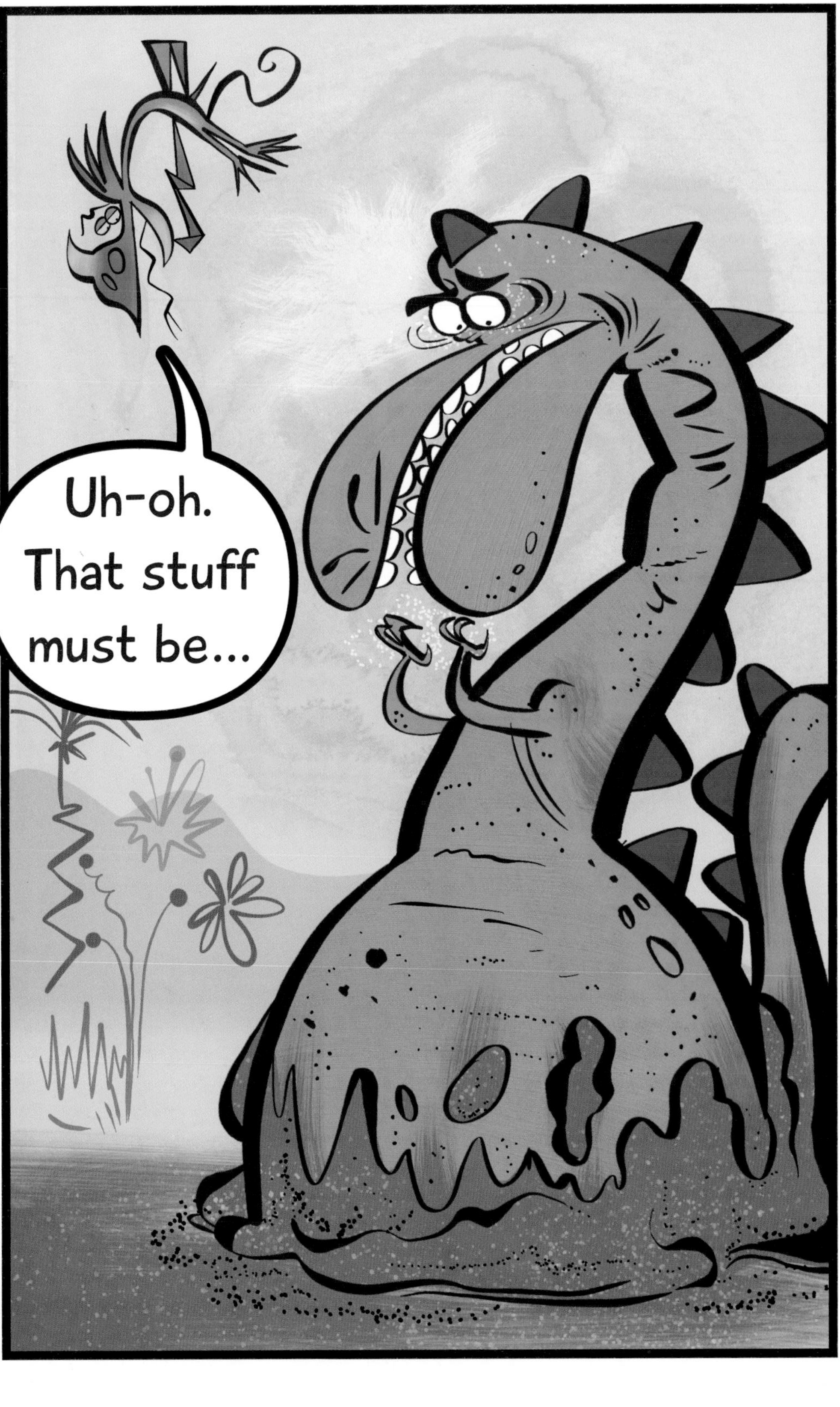
Uh-oh.
That stuff
must be...

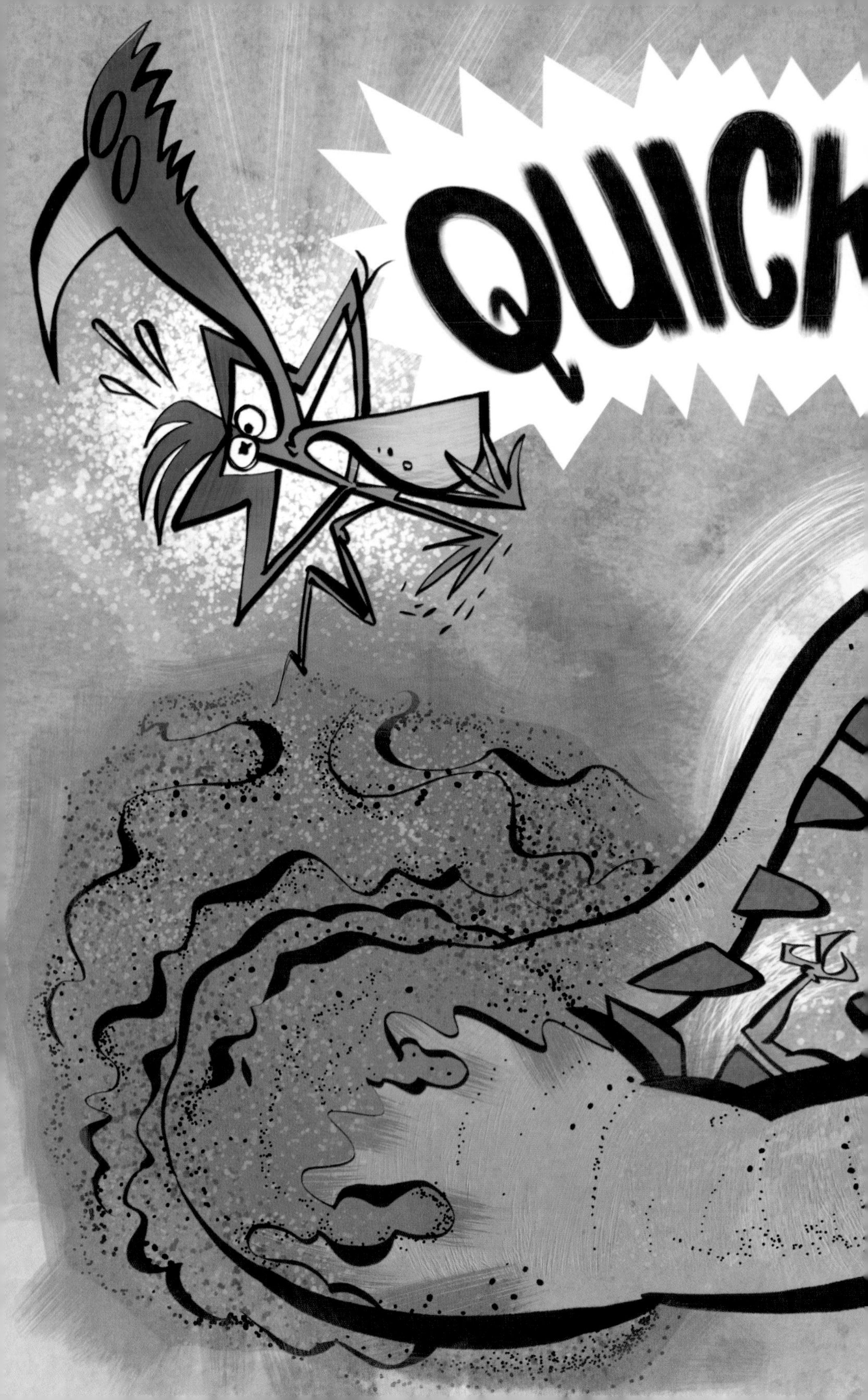
QUIC

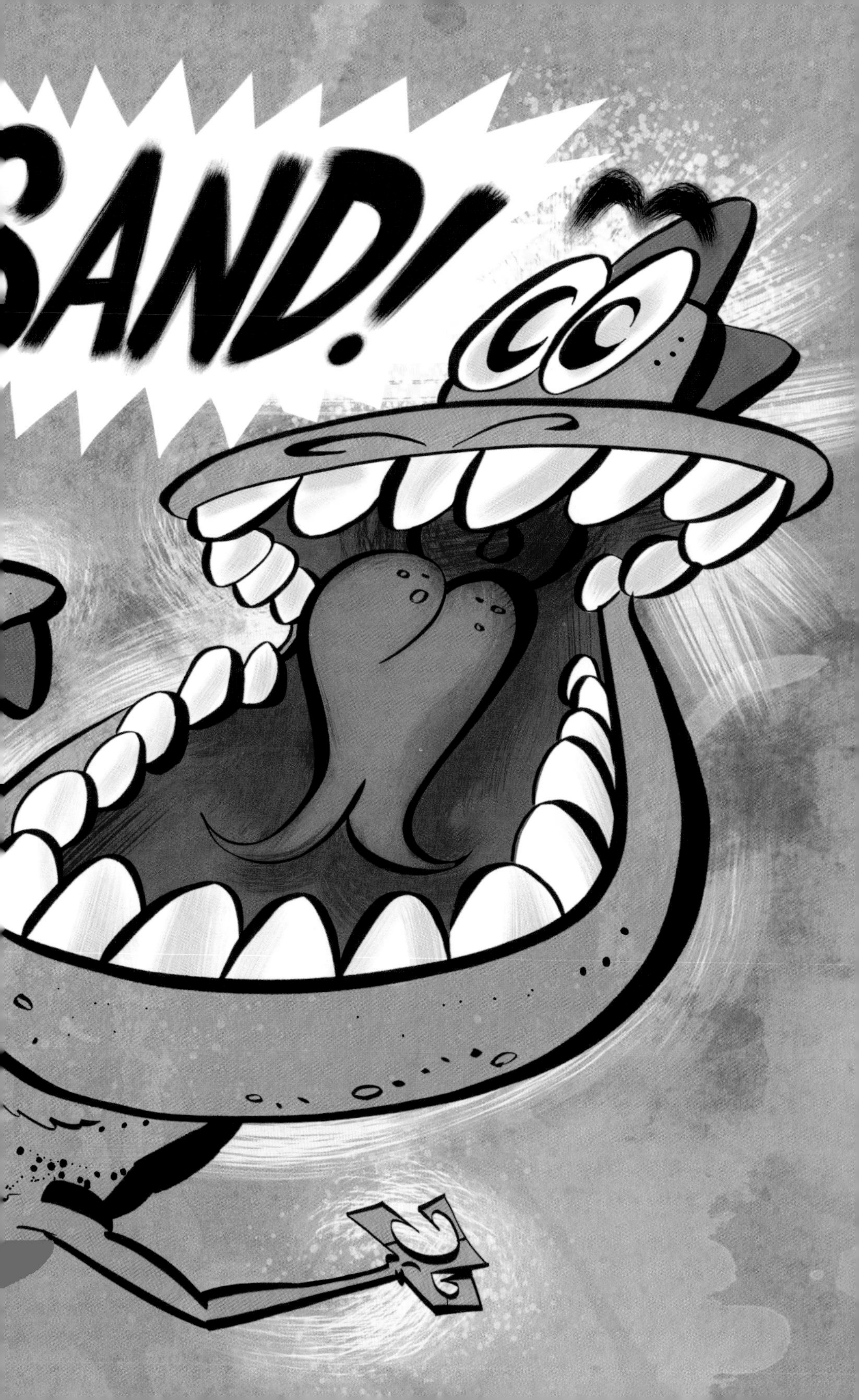
BAND!

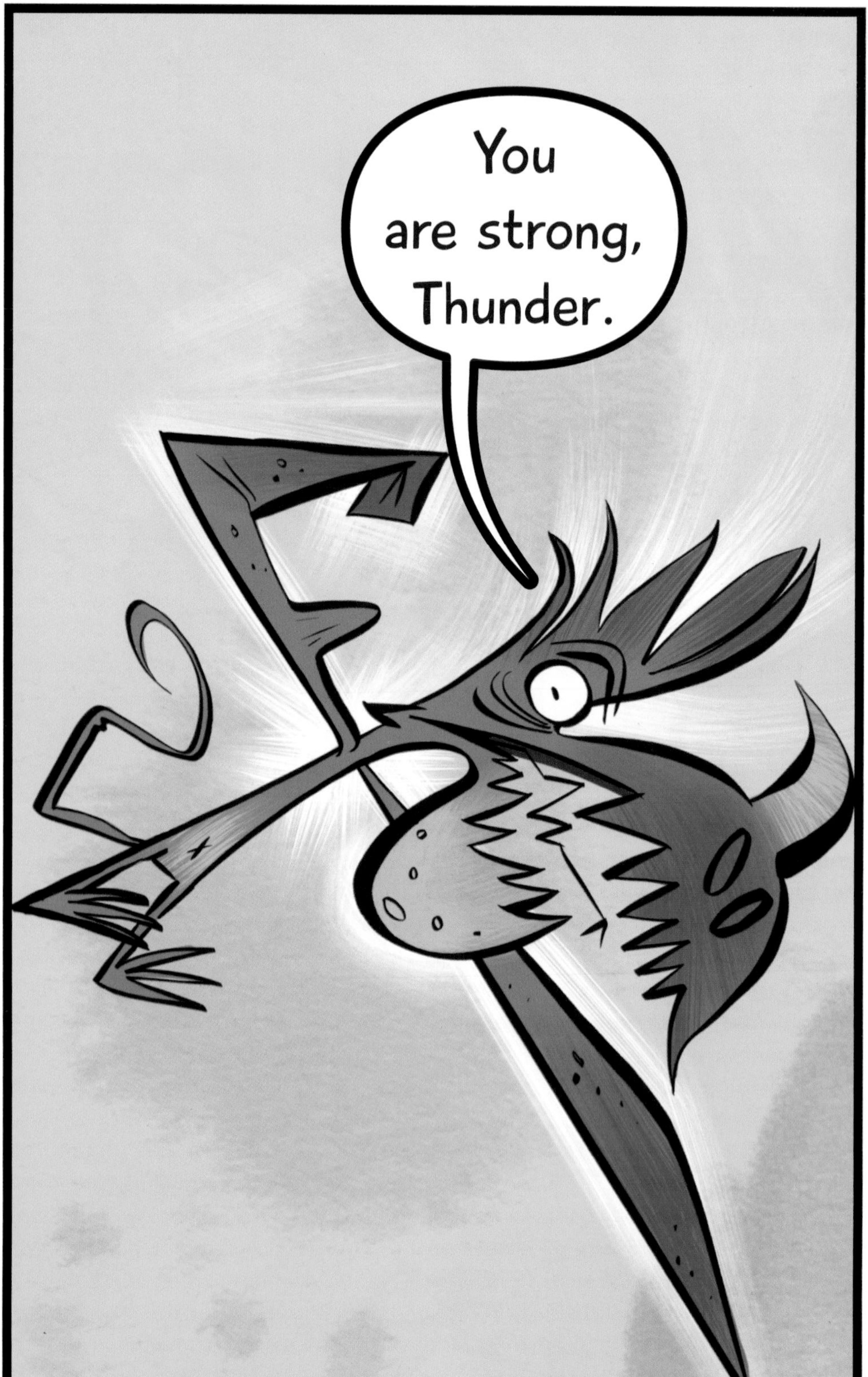
You are strong, Thunder.

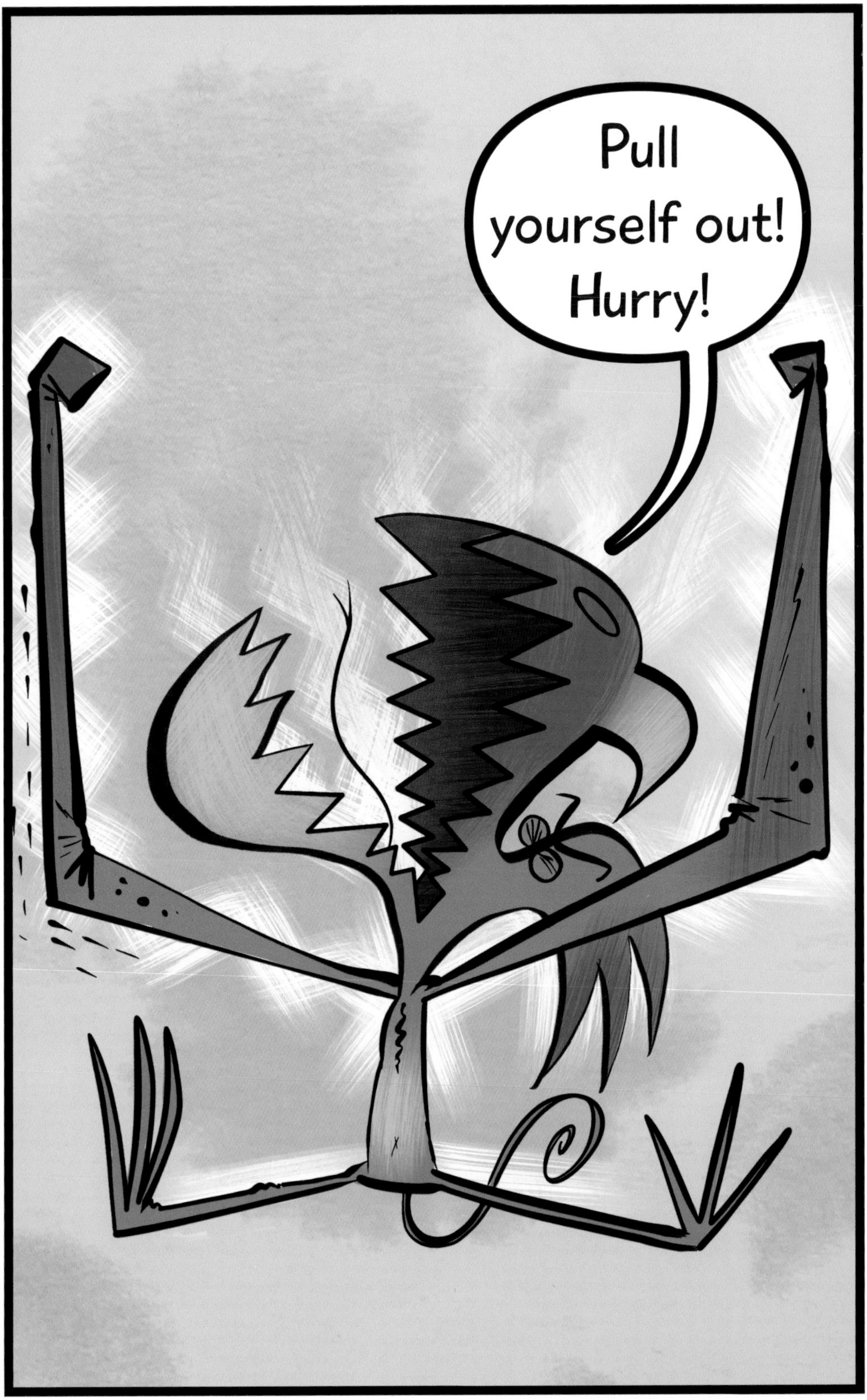
Pull yourself out! Hurry!

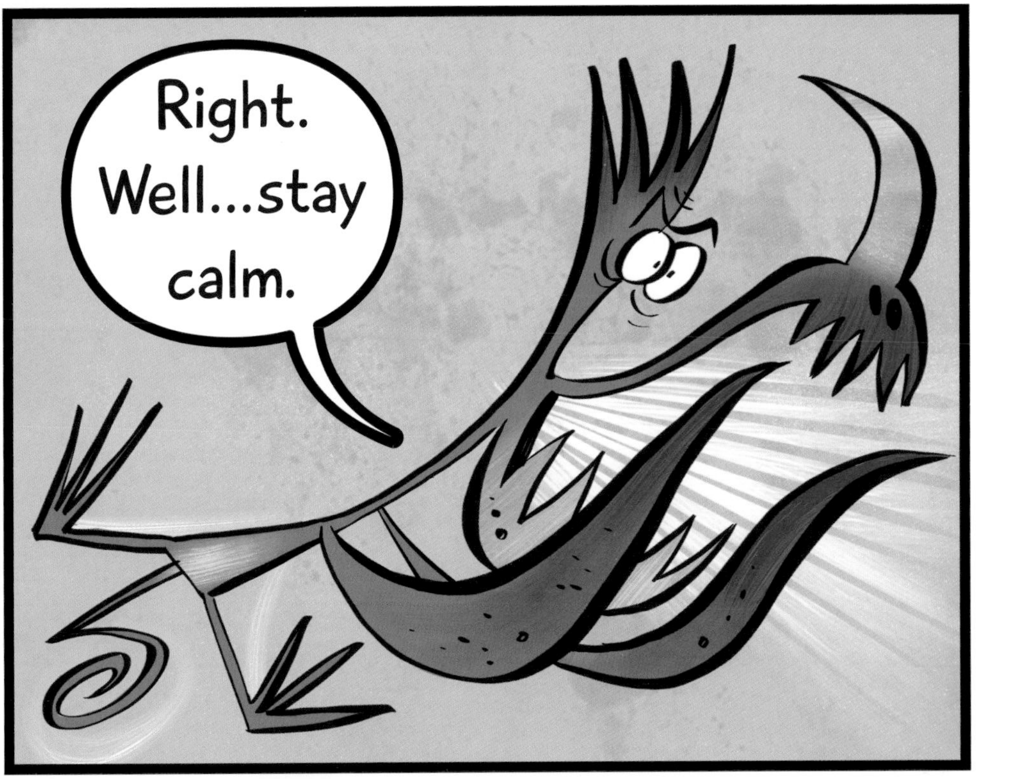
Right. Well...stay calm.

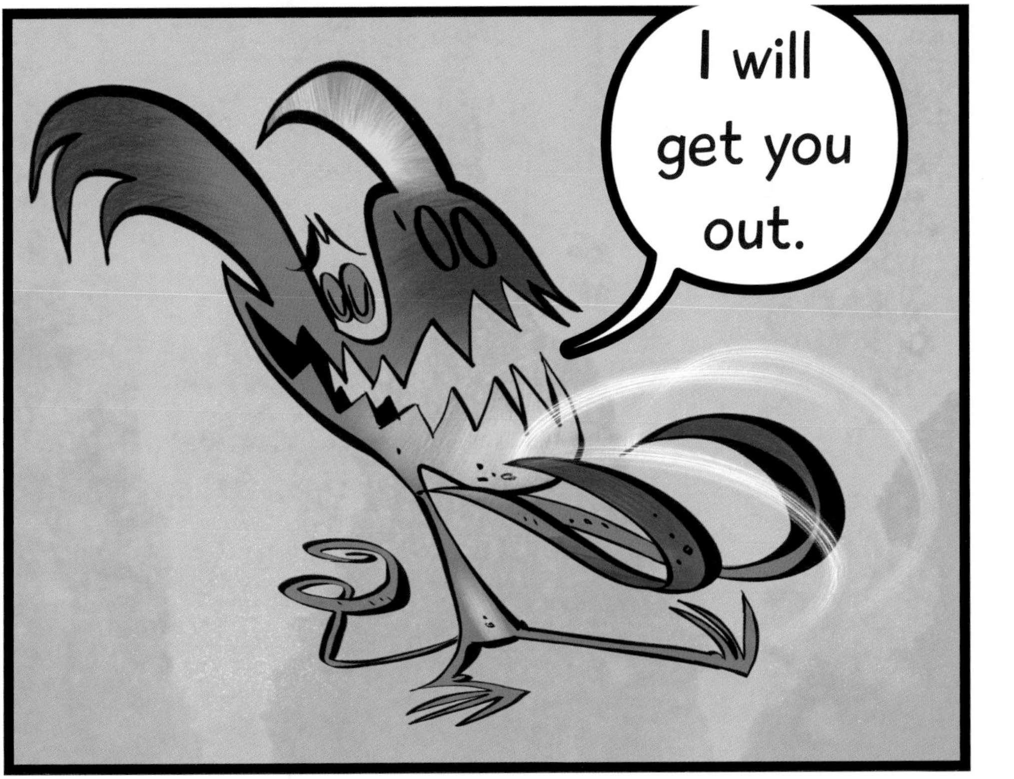
I will get you out.

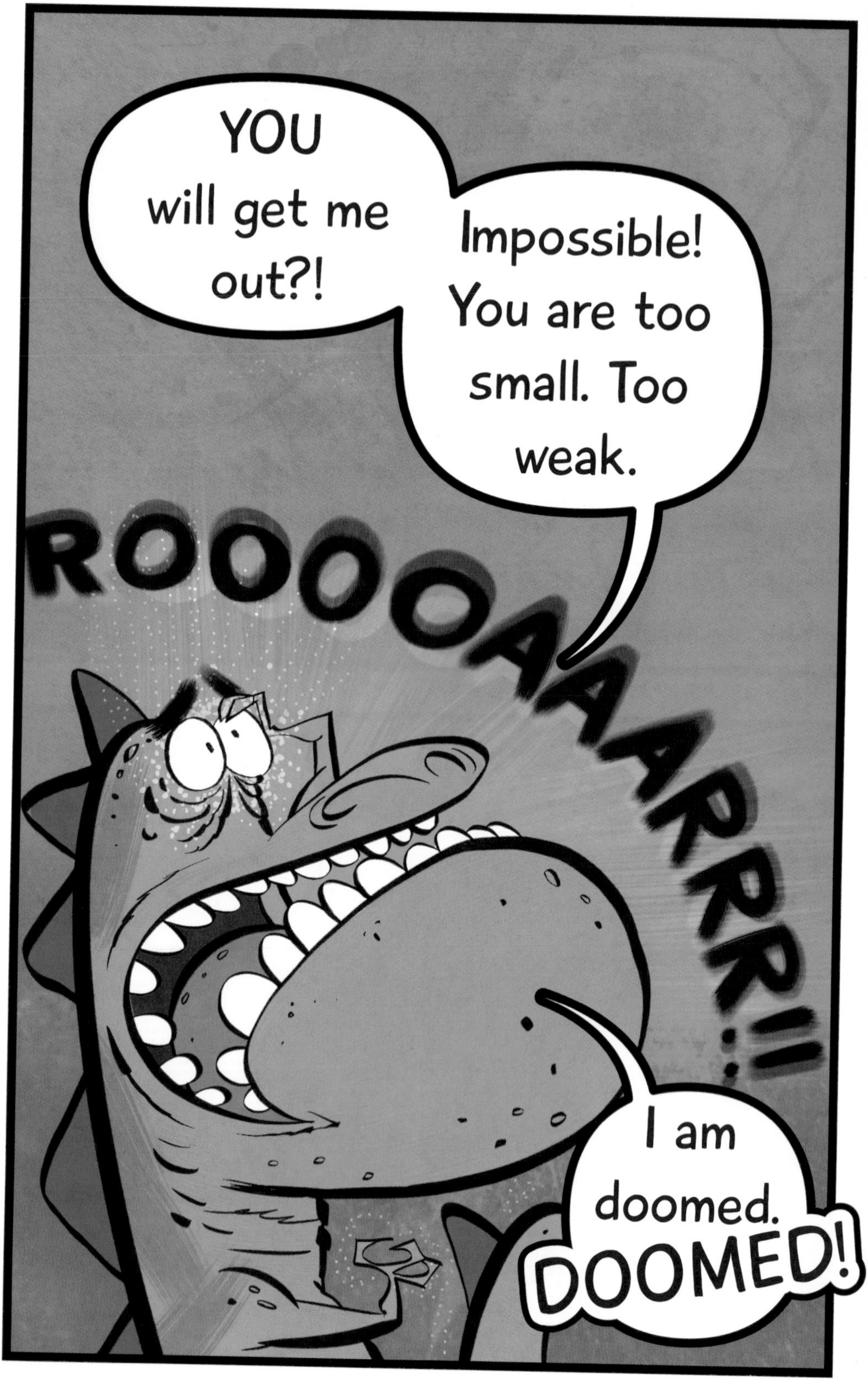
YOU will get me out?!
Impossible! You are too small. Too weak.
ROOOOAAAARRR!!
I am doomed. DOOMED!

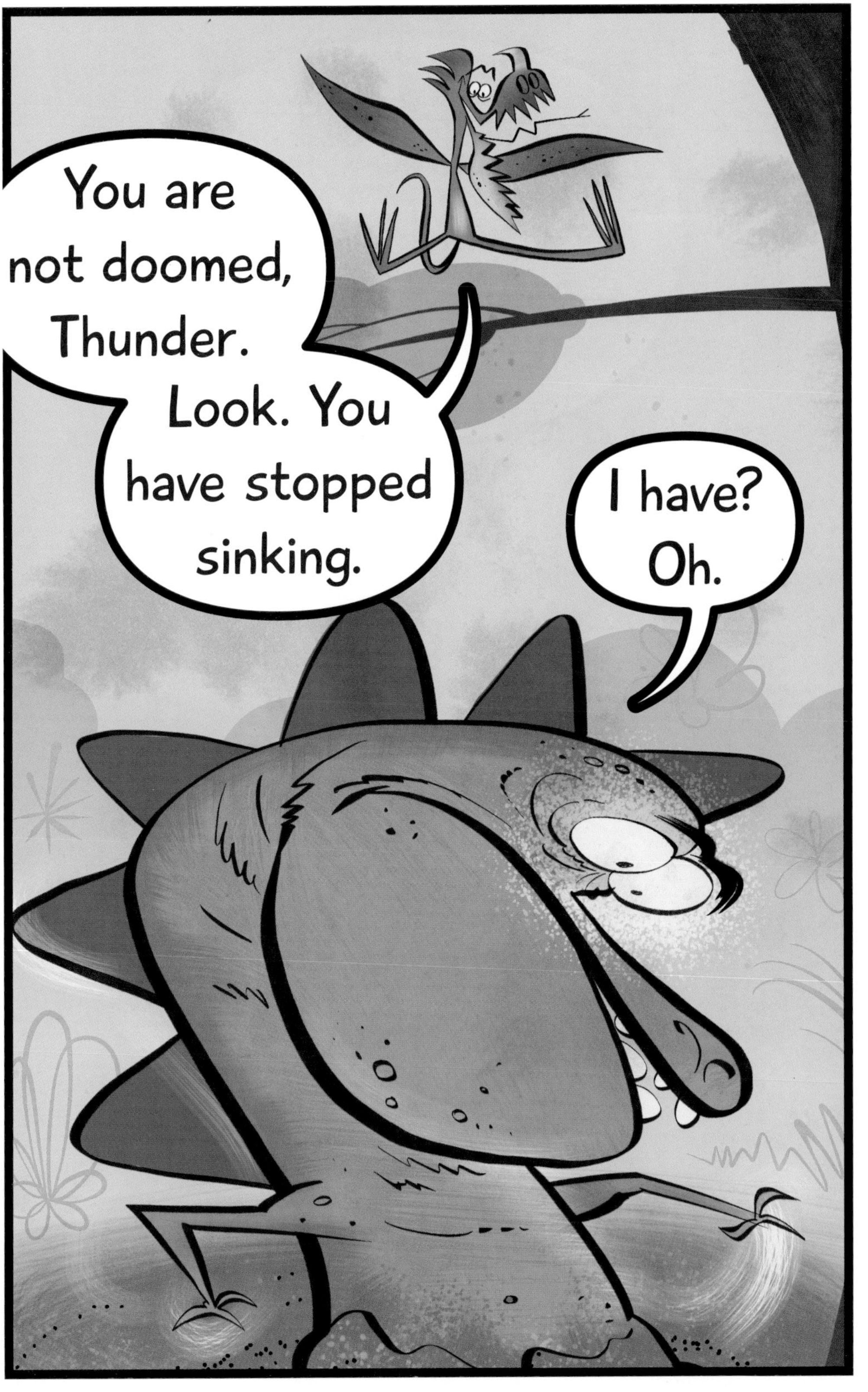
You are not doomed, Thunder. Look. You have stopped sinking.
I have? Oh.

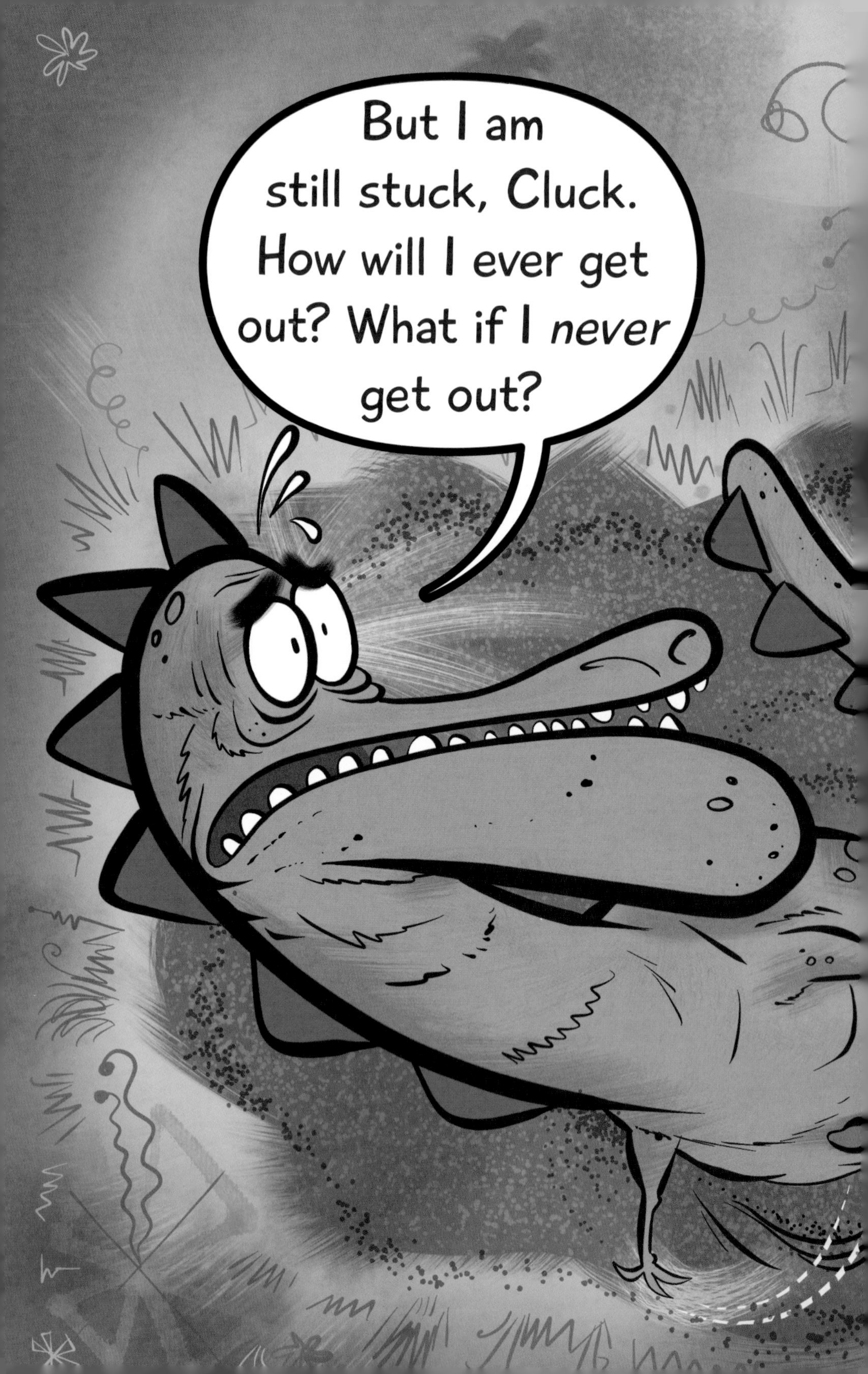
But I am still stuck, Cluck. How will I ever get out? What if I *never* get out?

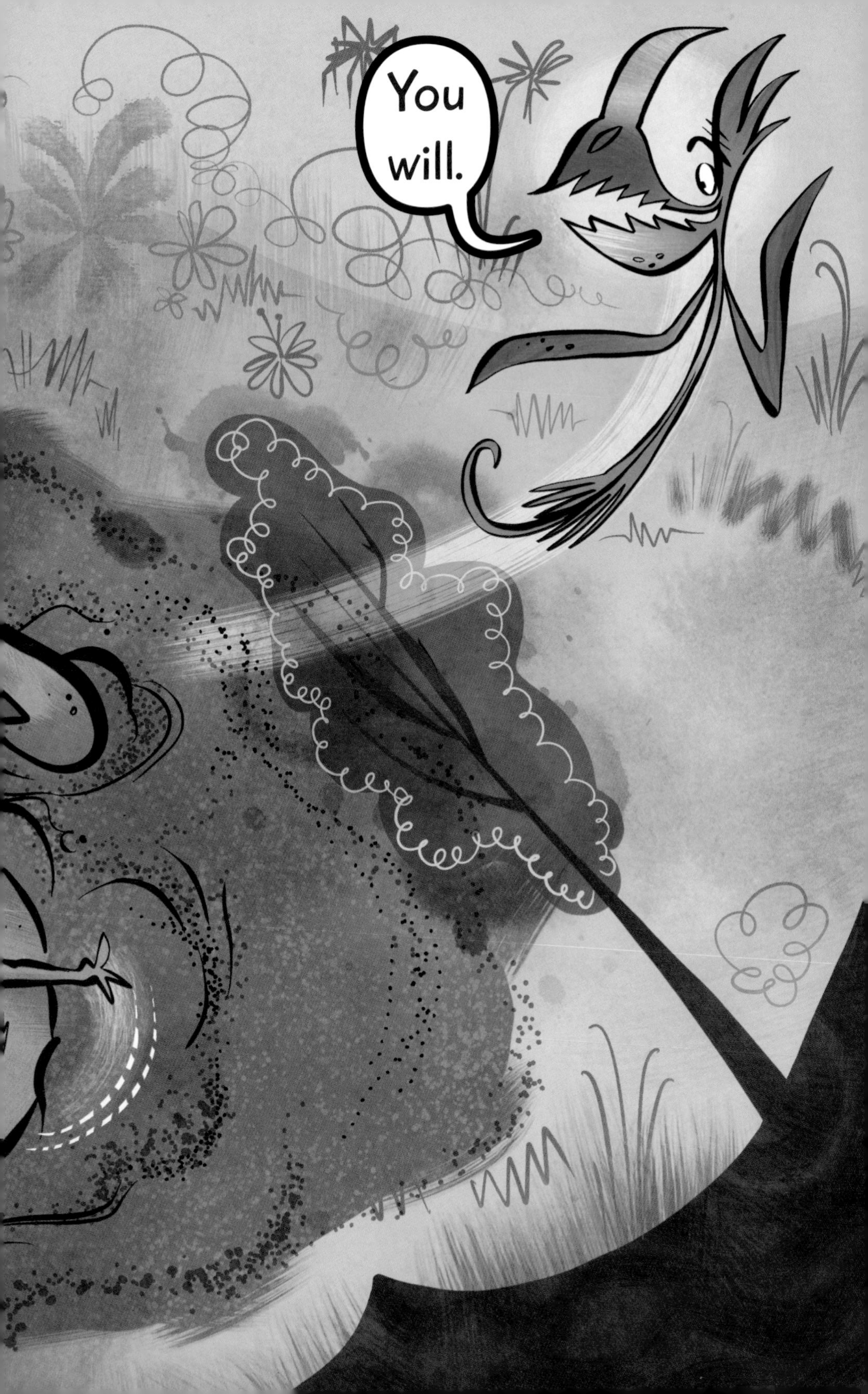
You will.

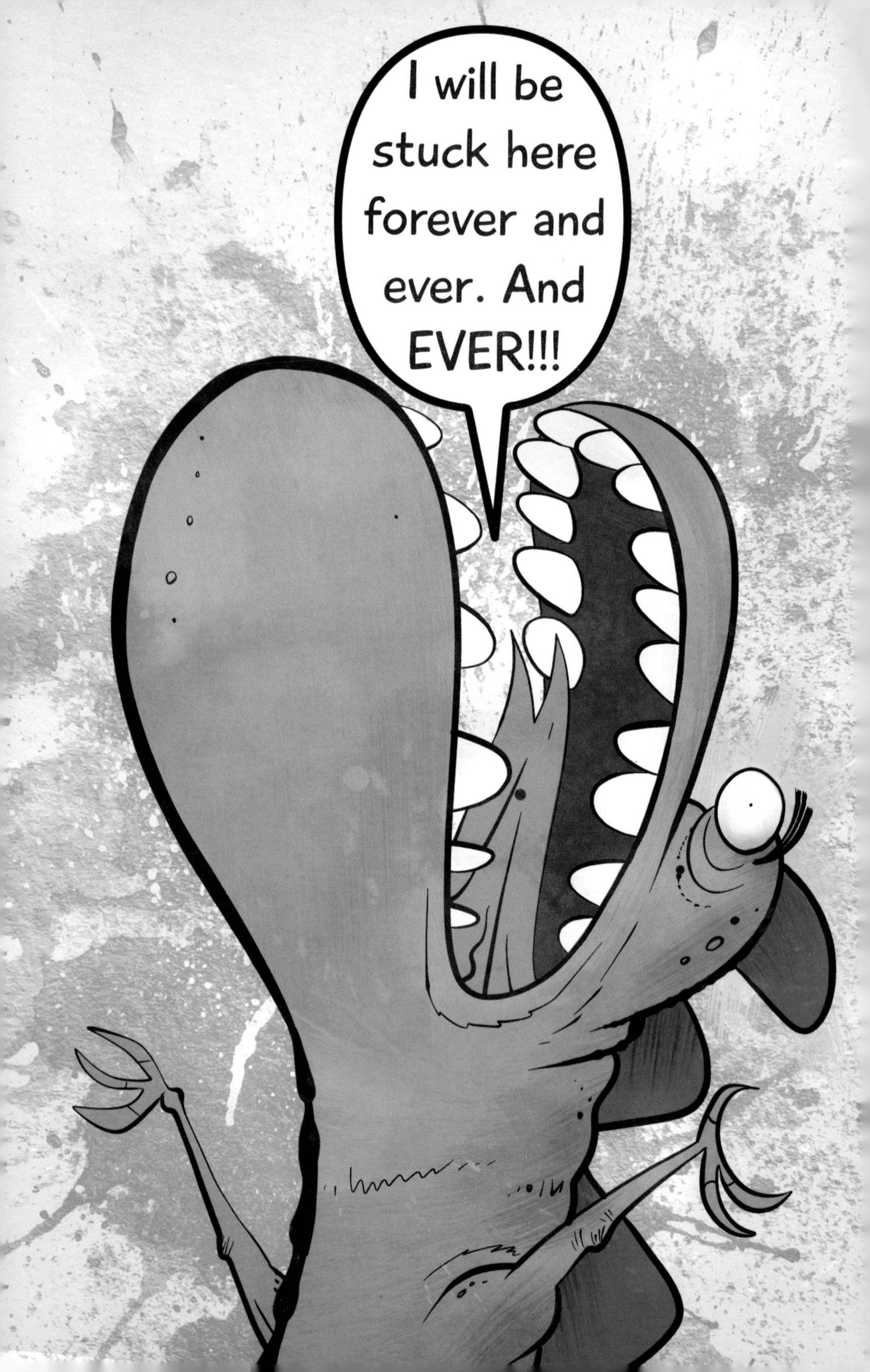
I will be stuck here forever and ever. And EVER!!!

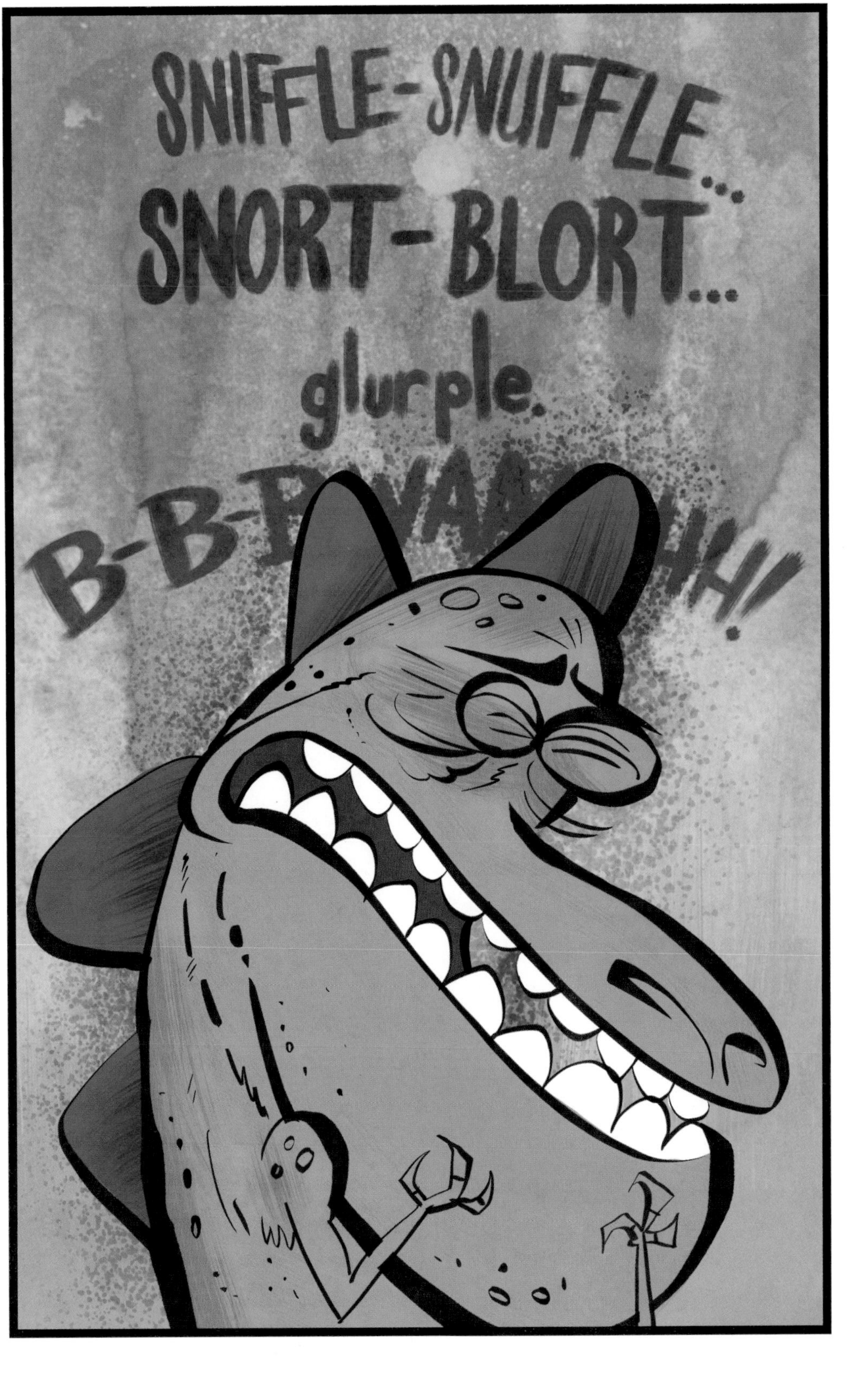
SNIFFLE-SNUFFLE...
SNORT-BLORT...
glurple.

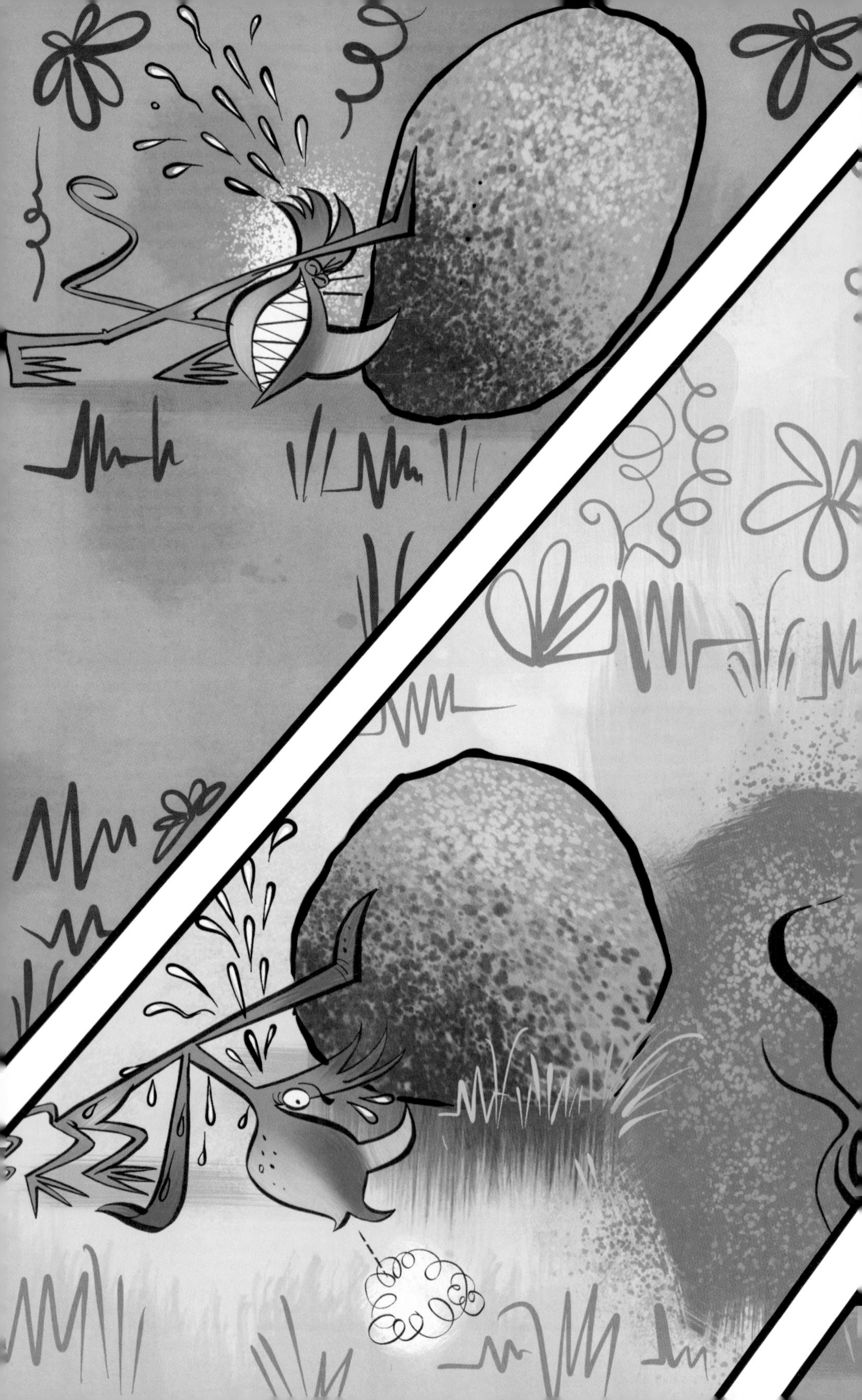

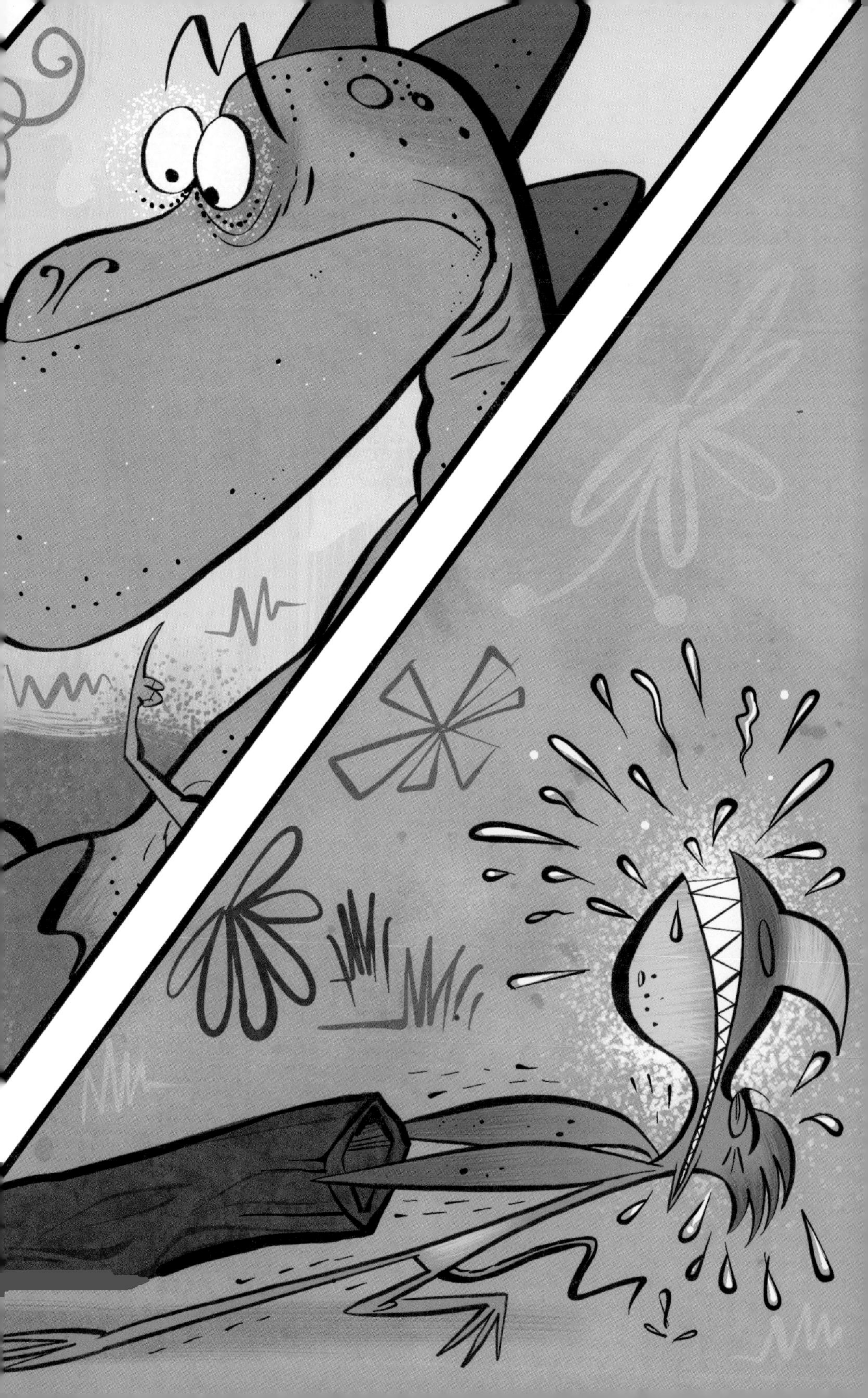

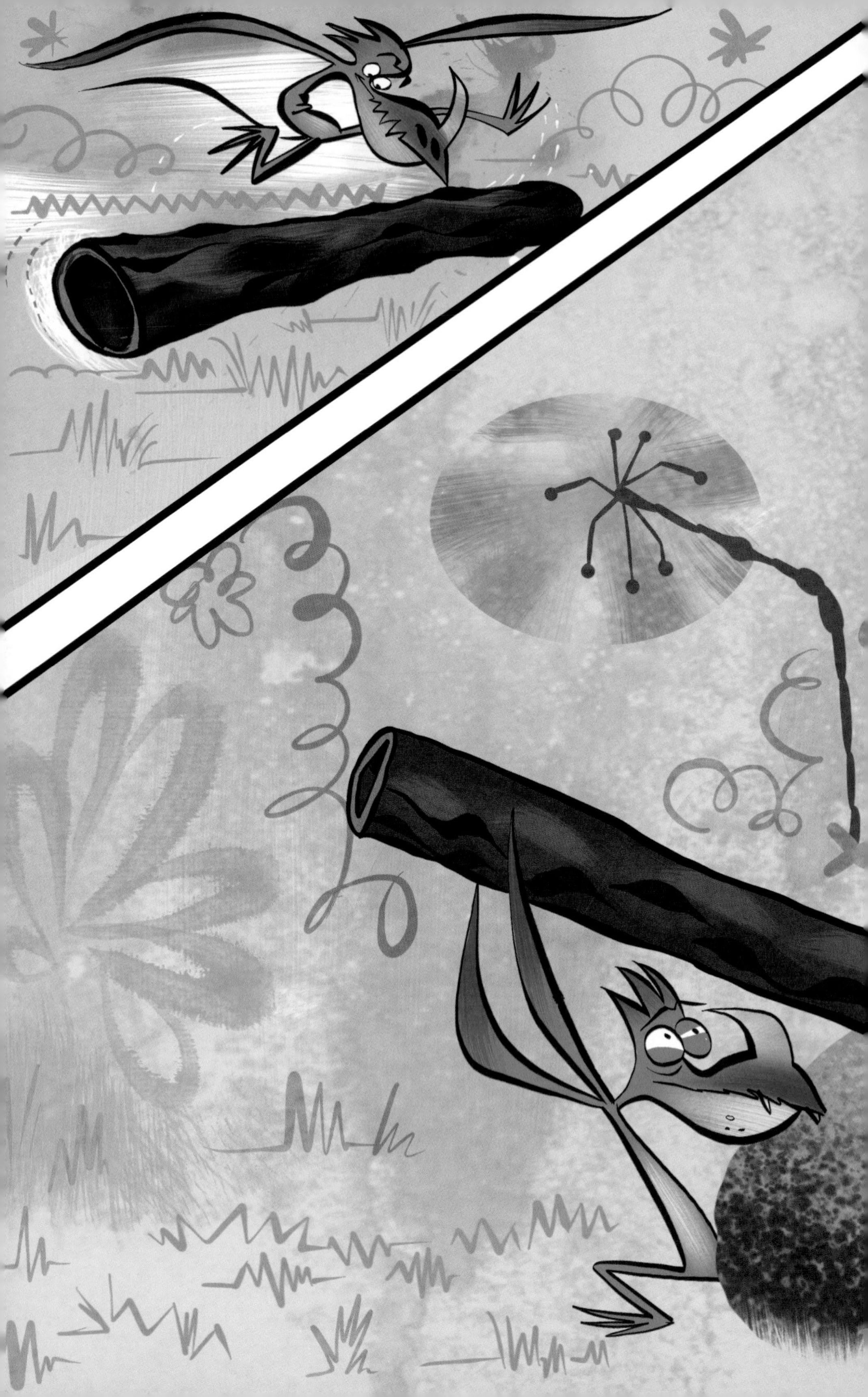

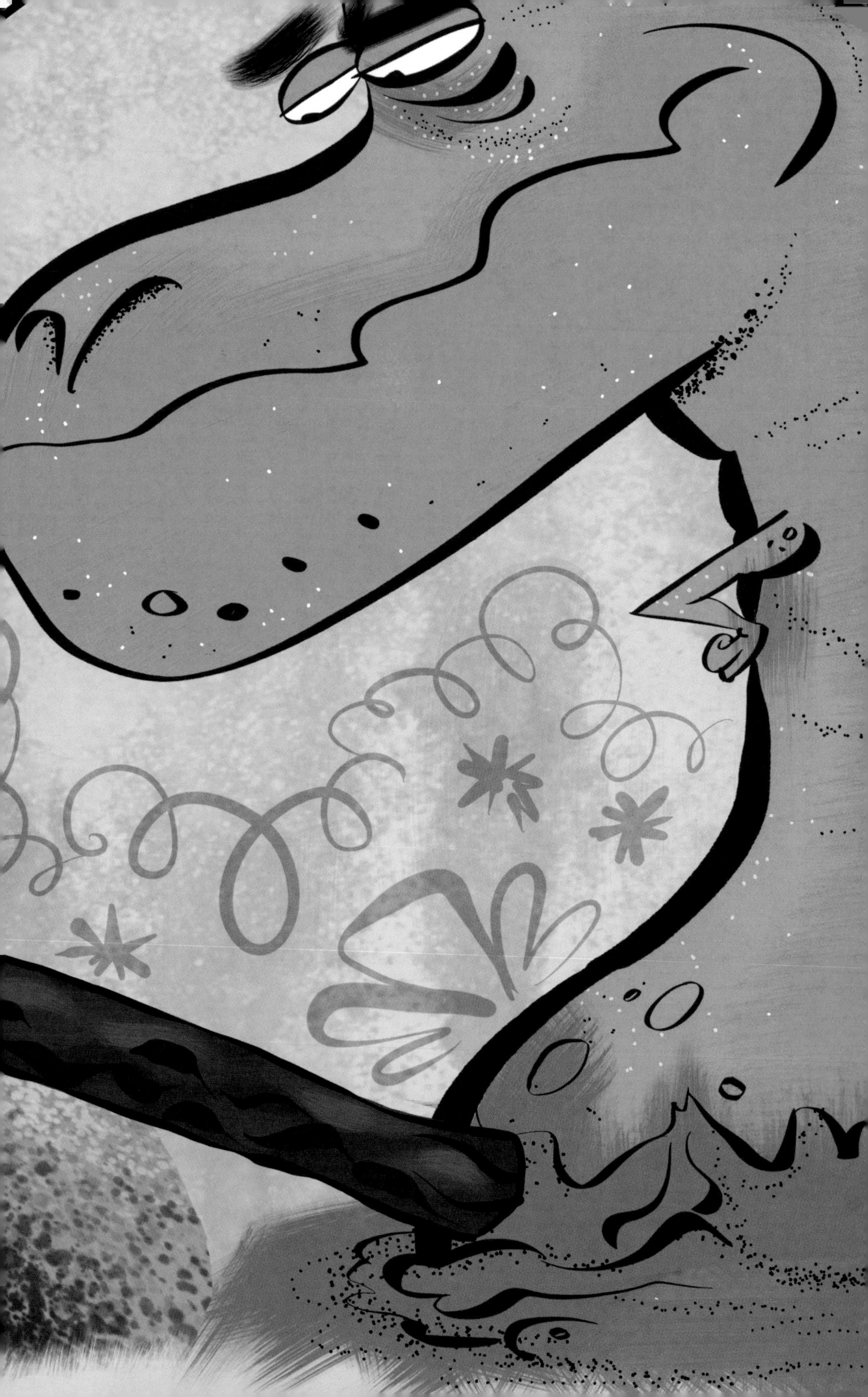

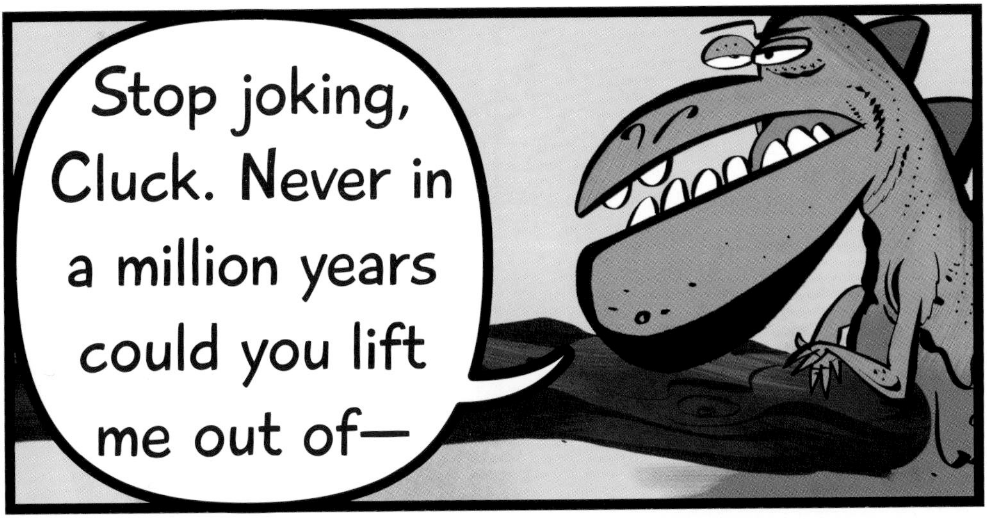
Stop joking, Cluck. Never in a million years could you lift me out of—

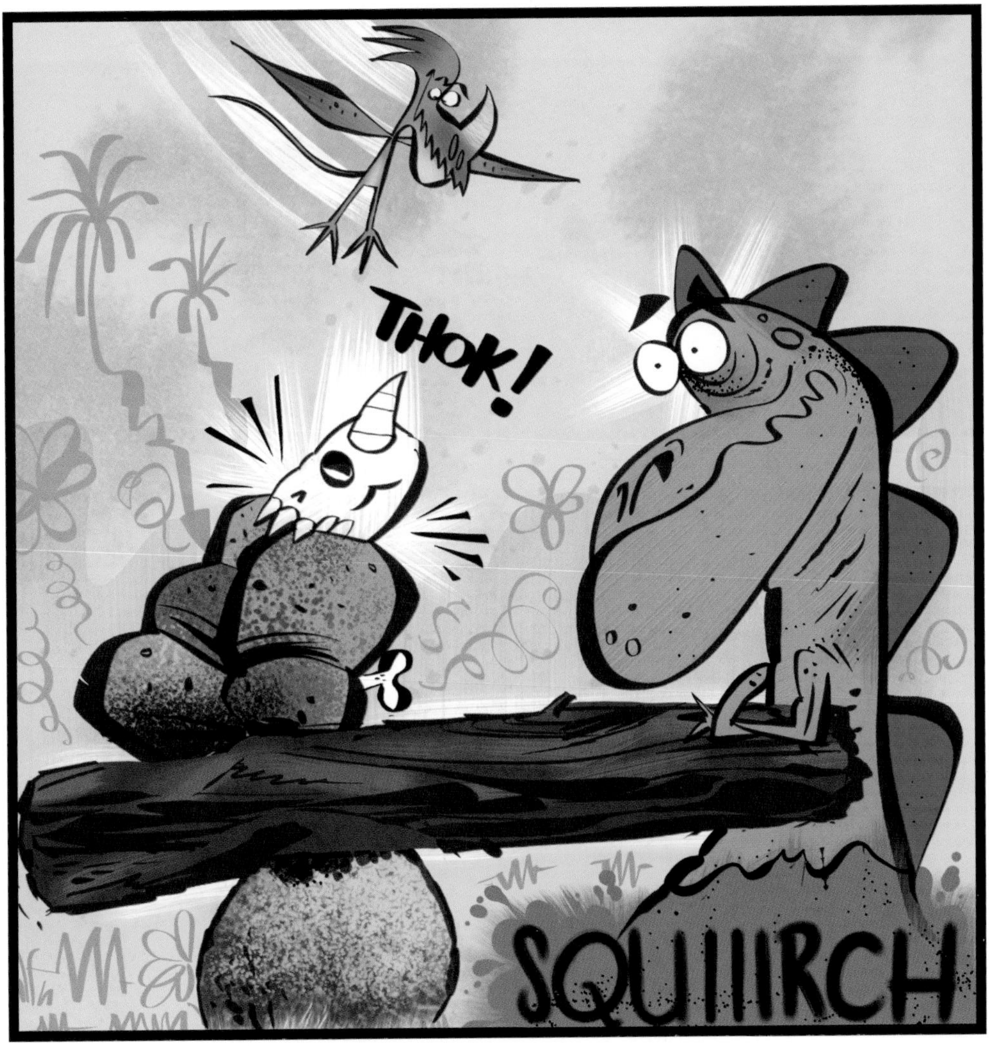
THOK!
SQUIIIRCH

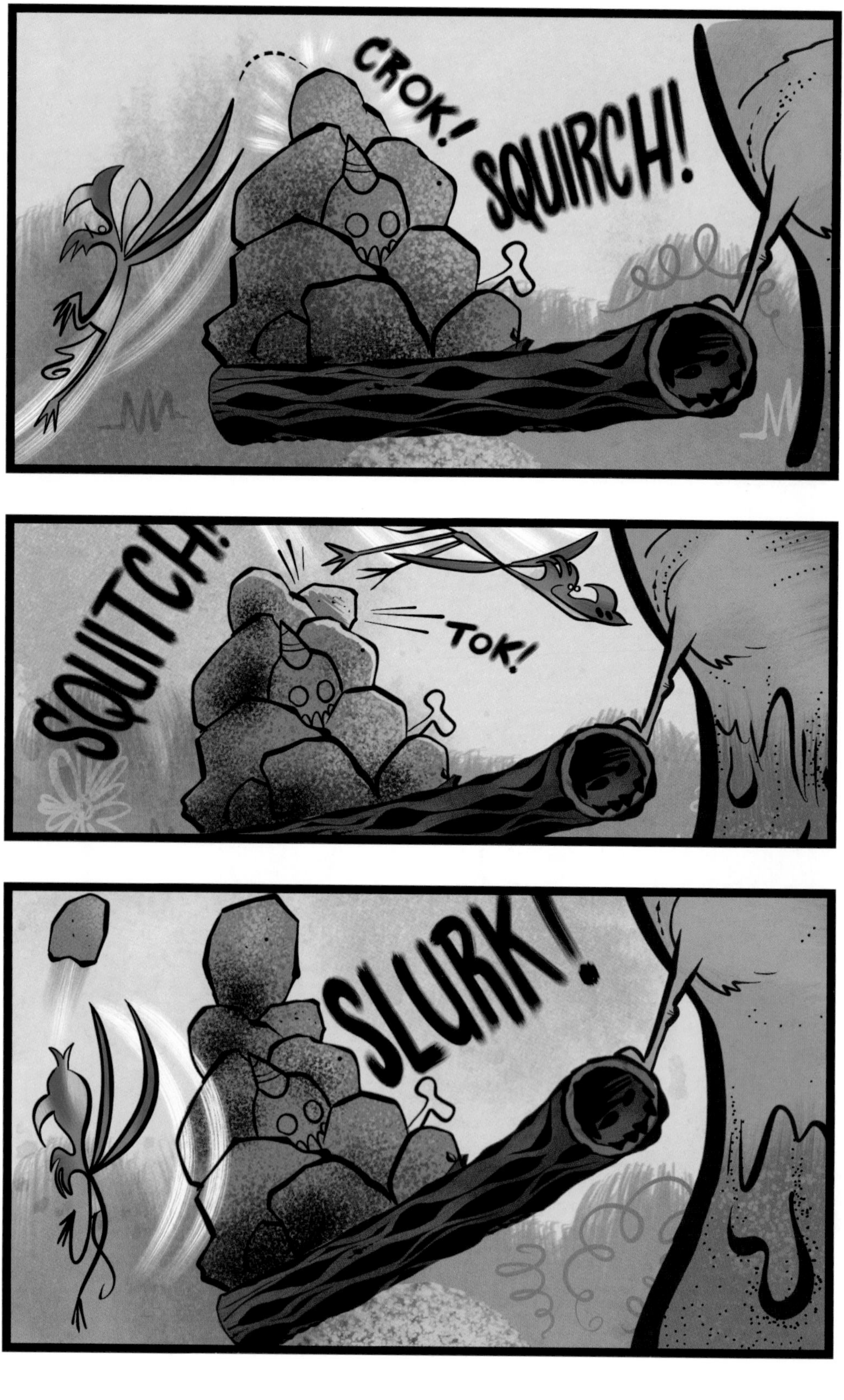
CROK!
SQUIRCH!
SQUITCH!
TOK!
SLURK!

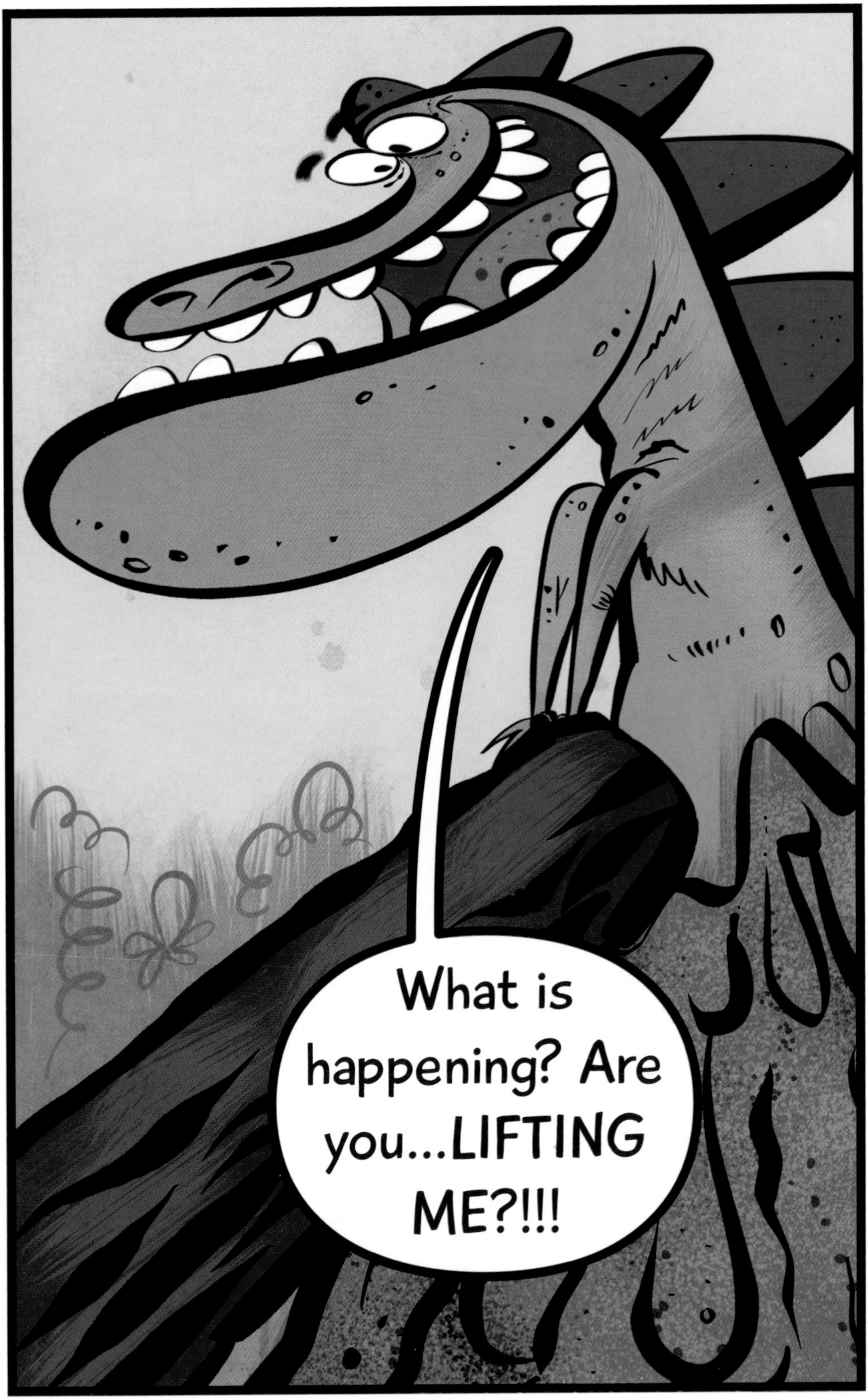
What is happening? Are you...LIFTING ME?!!!

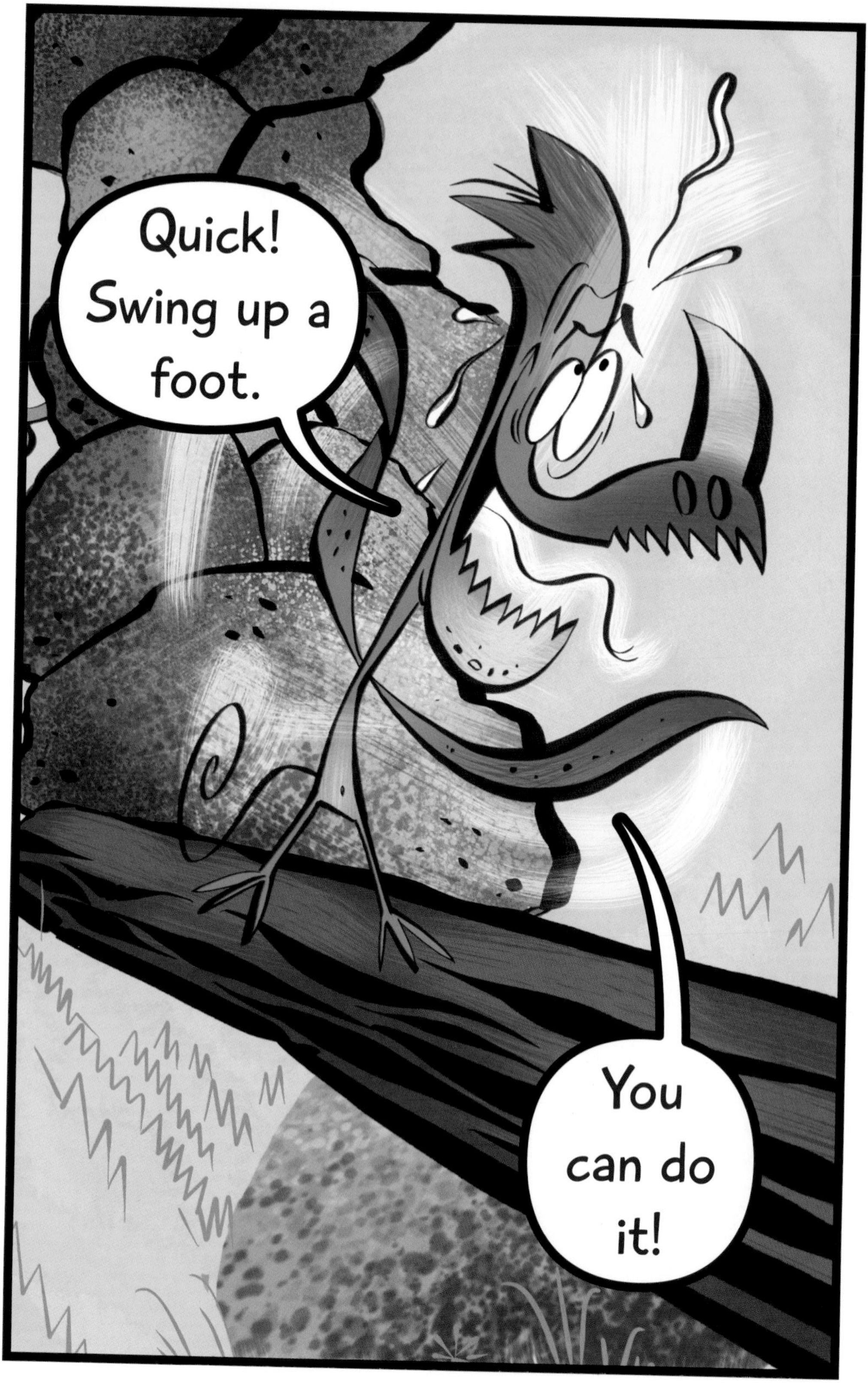
Quick! Swing up a foot.
You can do it!

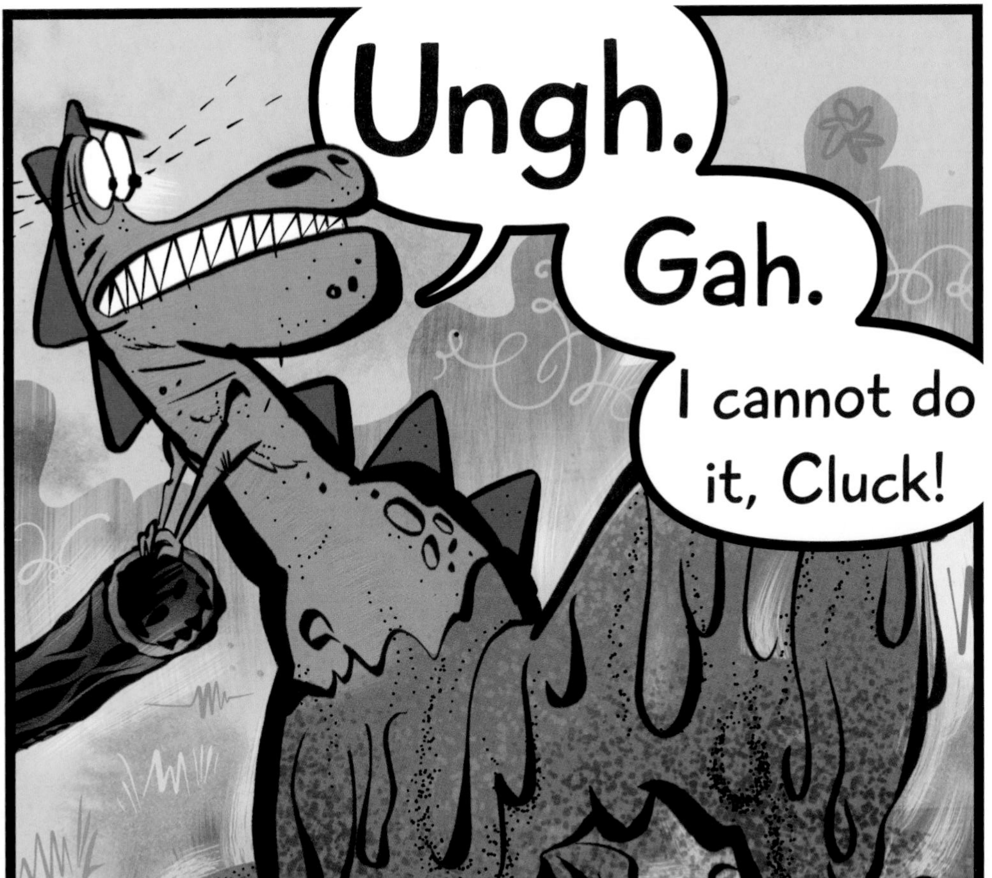
Ungh.
Gah.
I cannot do it, Cluck!

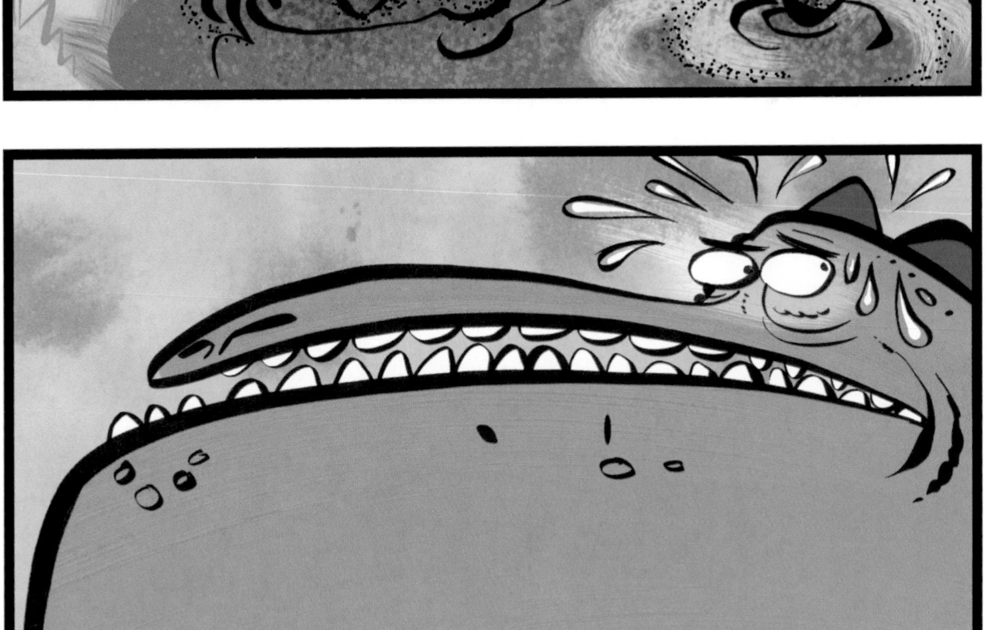

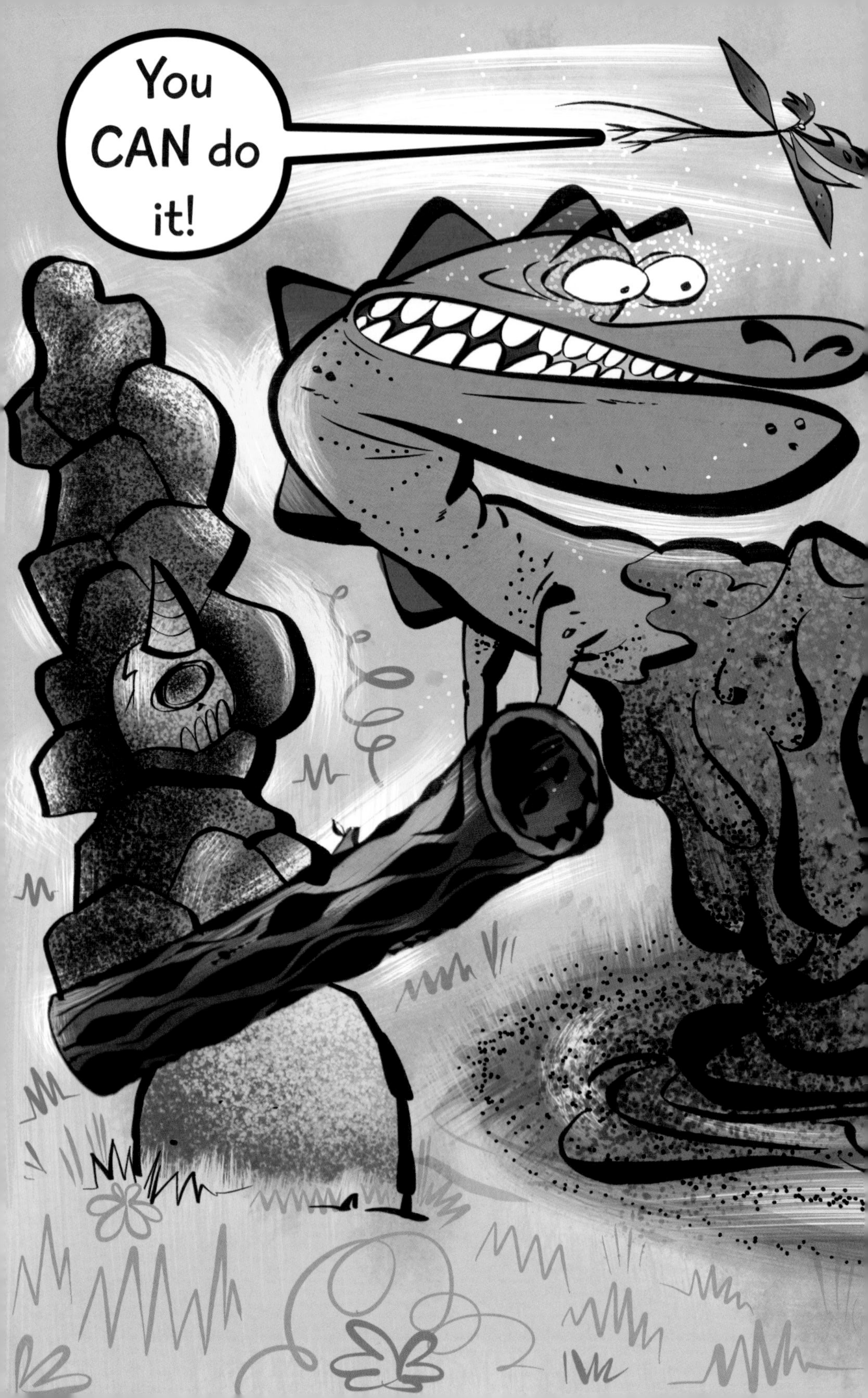
You CAN do it!

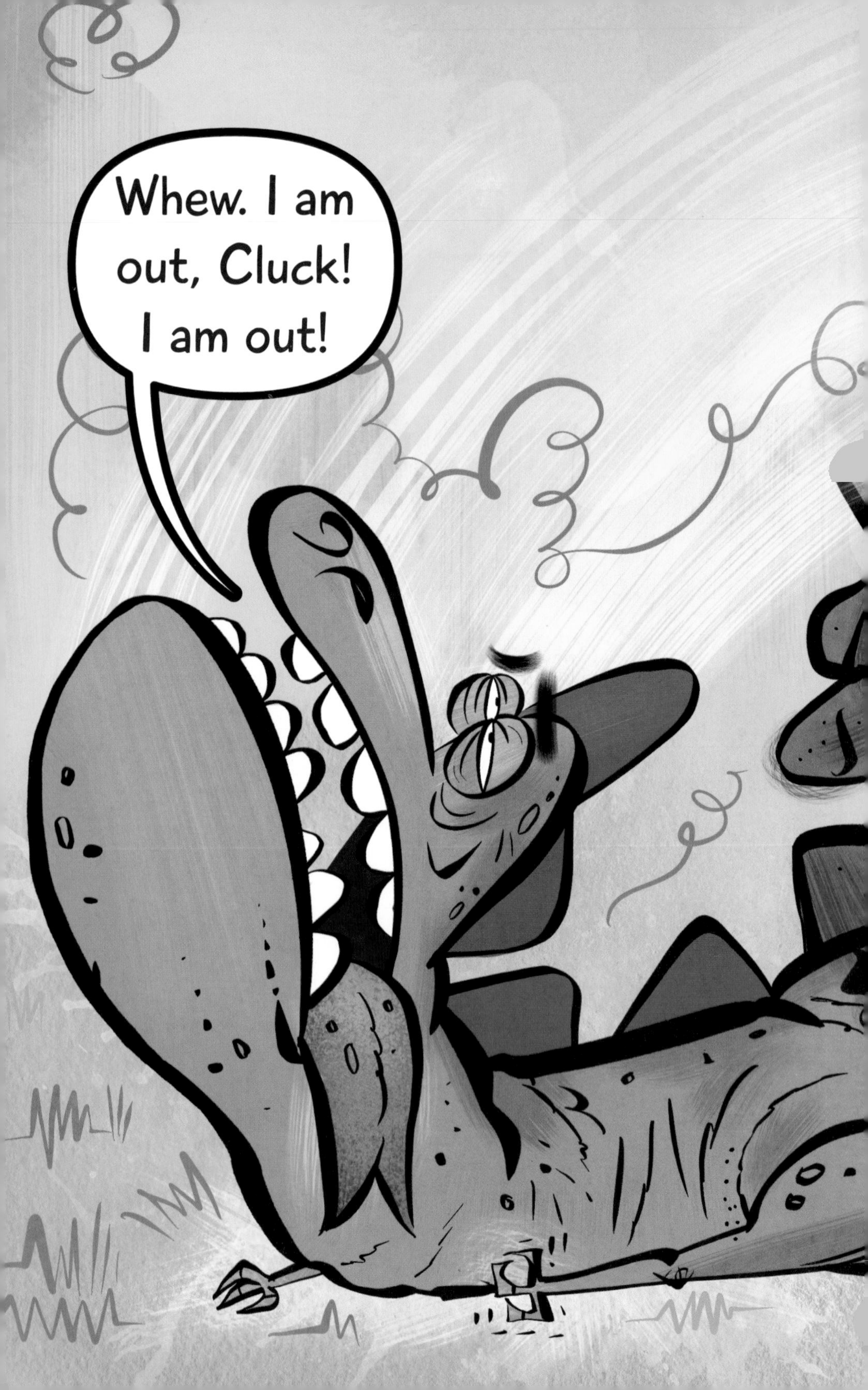
Whew. I am out, Cluck! I am out!

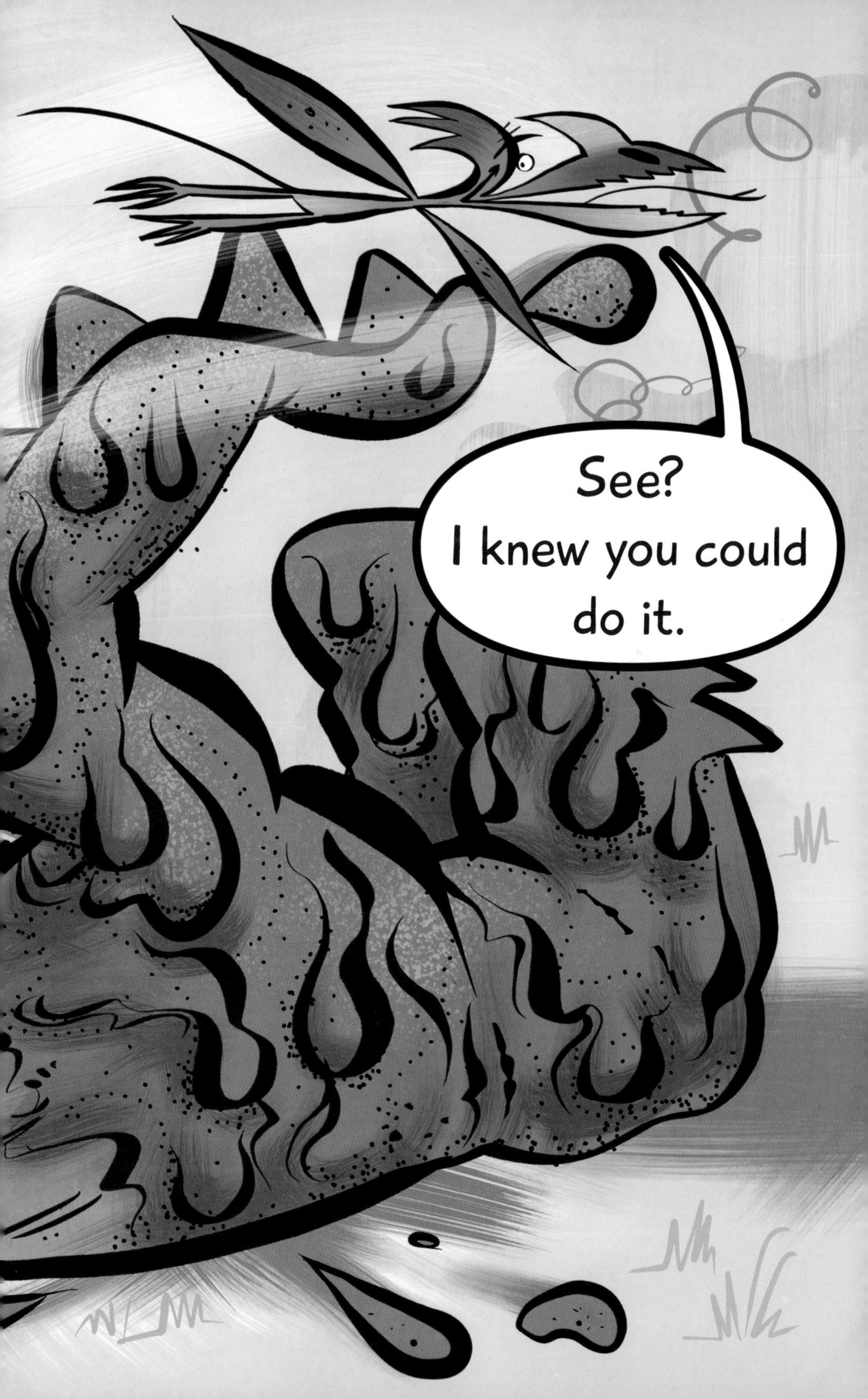
See?
I knew you could do it.

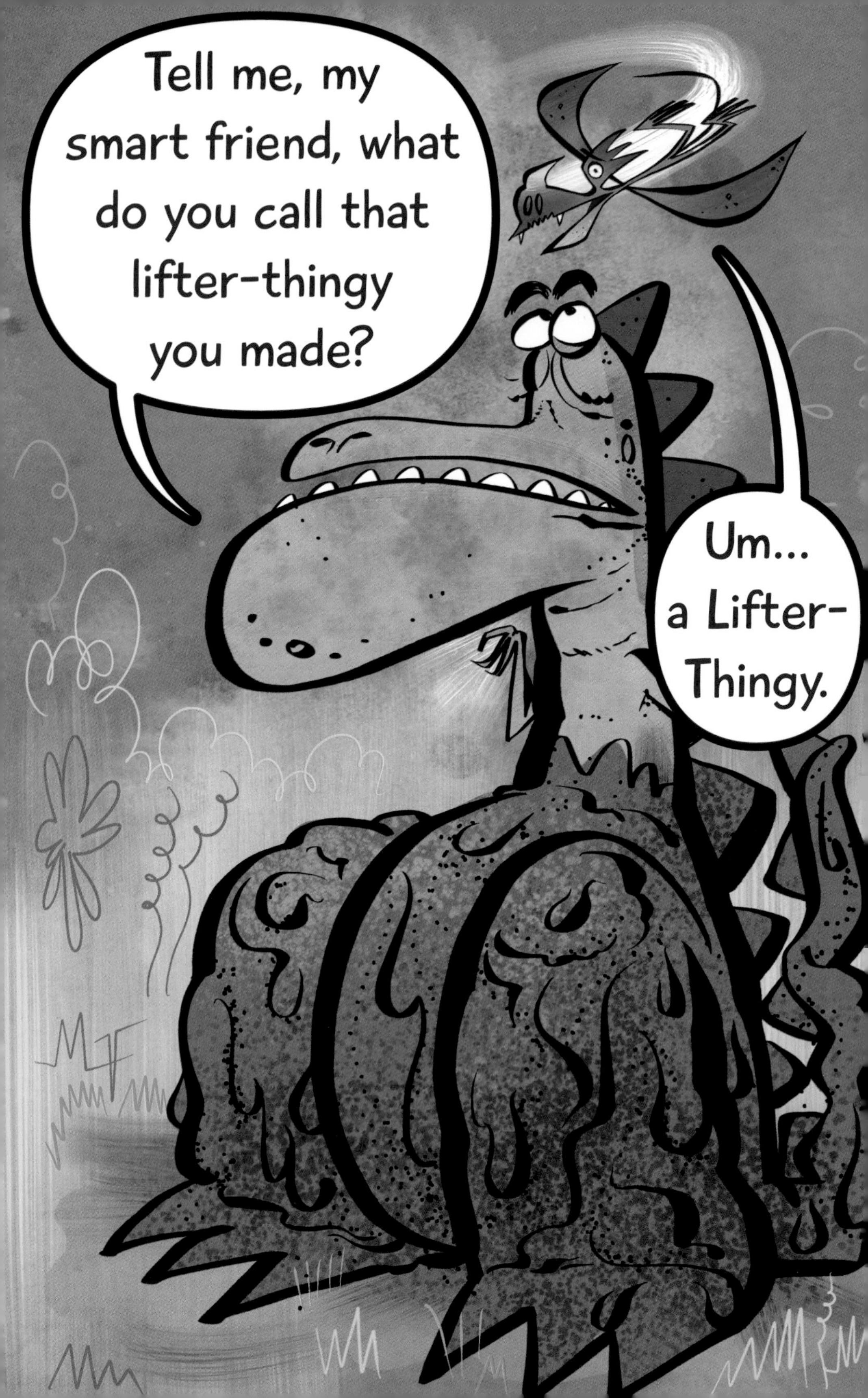
Tell me, my smart friend, what do you call that lifter-thingy you made?
Um... a Lifter-Thingy.

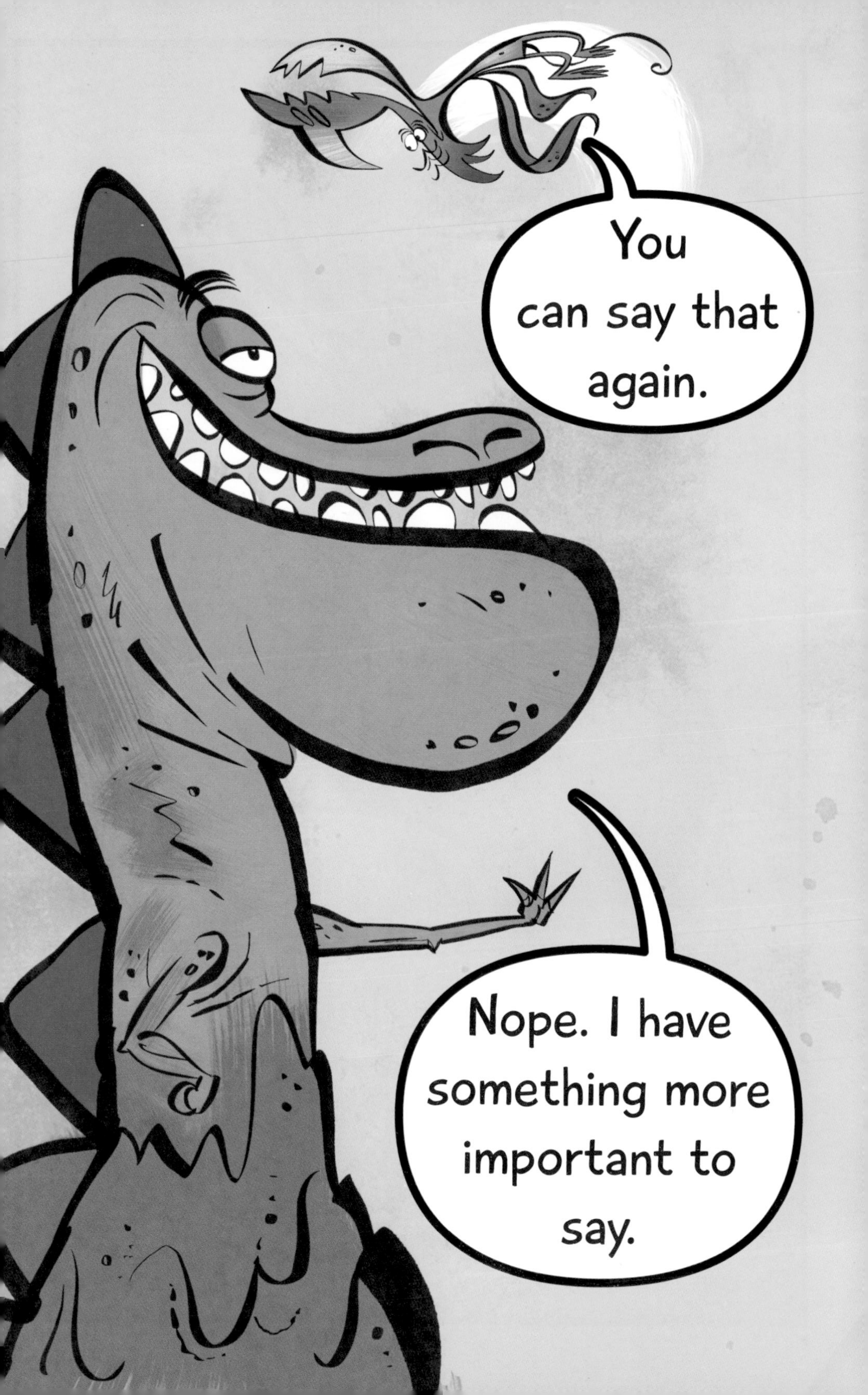
You can say that again.
Nope. I have something more important to say.

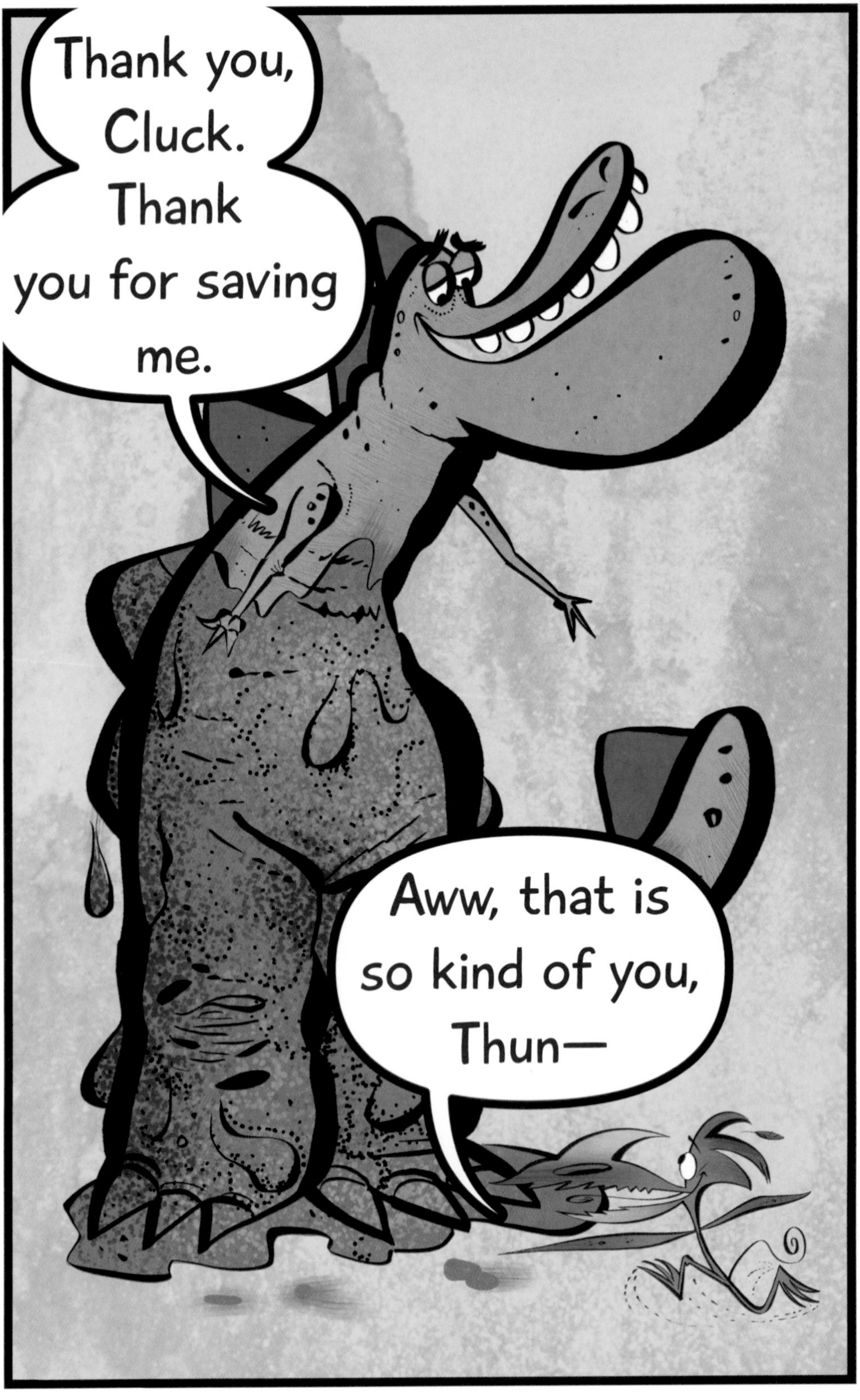
Thank you, Cluck. Thank you for saving me.
Aww, that is so kind of you, Thun—

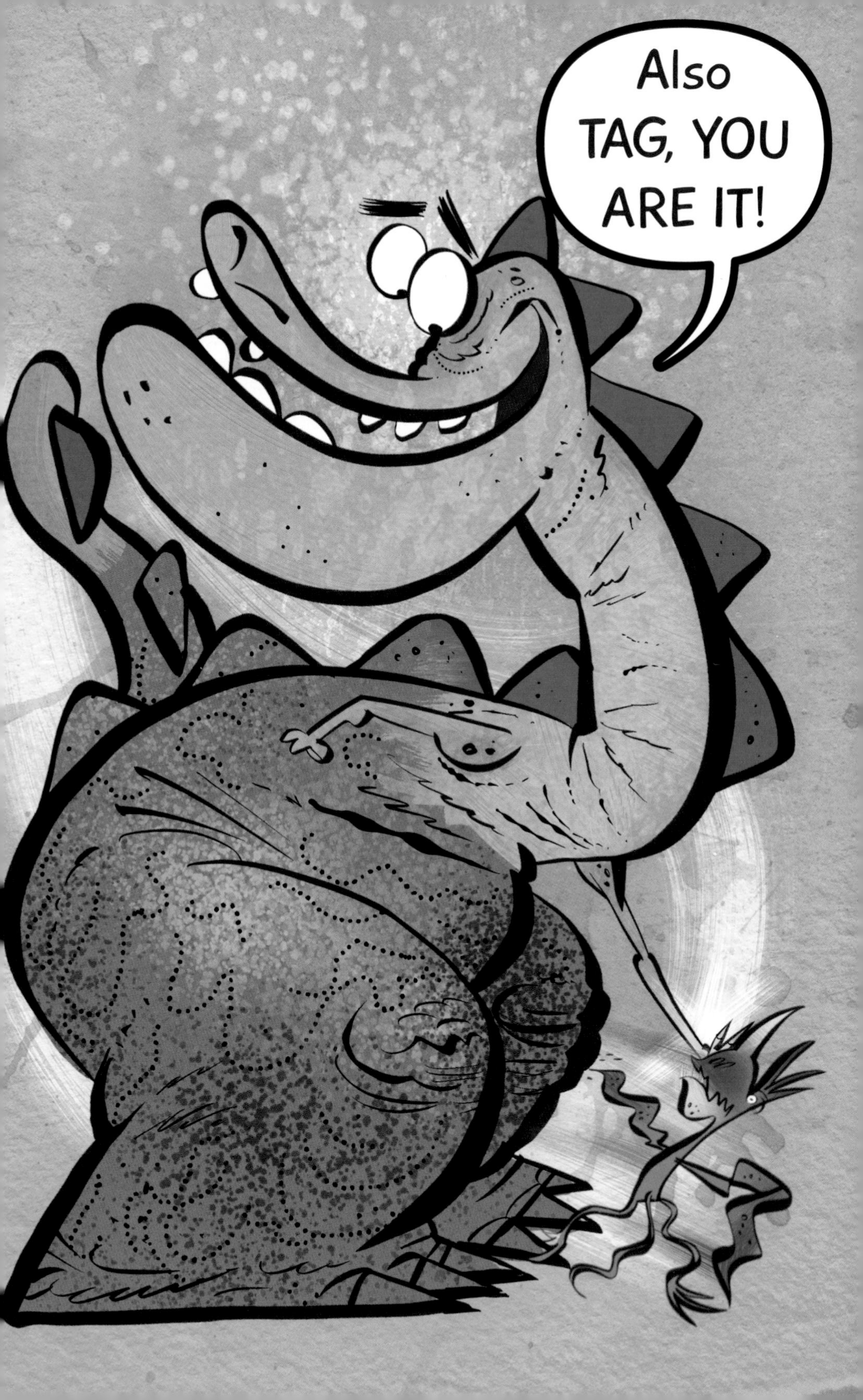
Also TAG, YOU ARE IT!

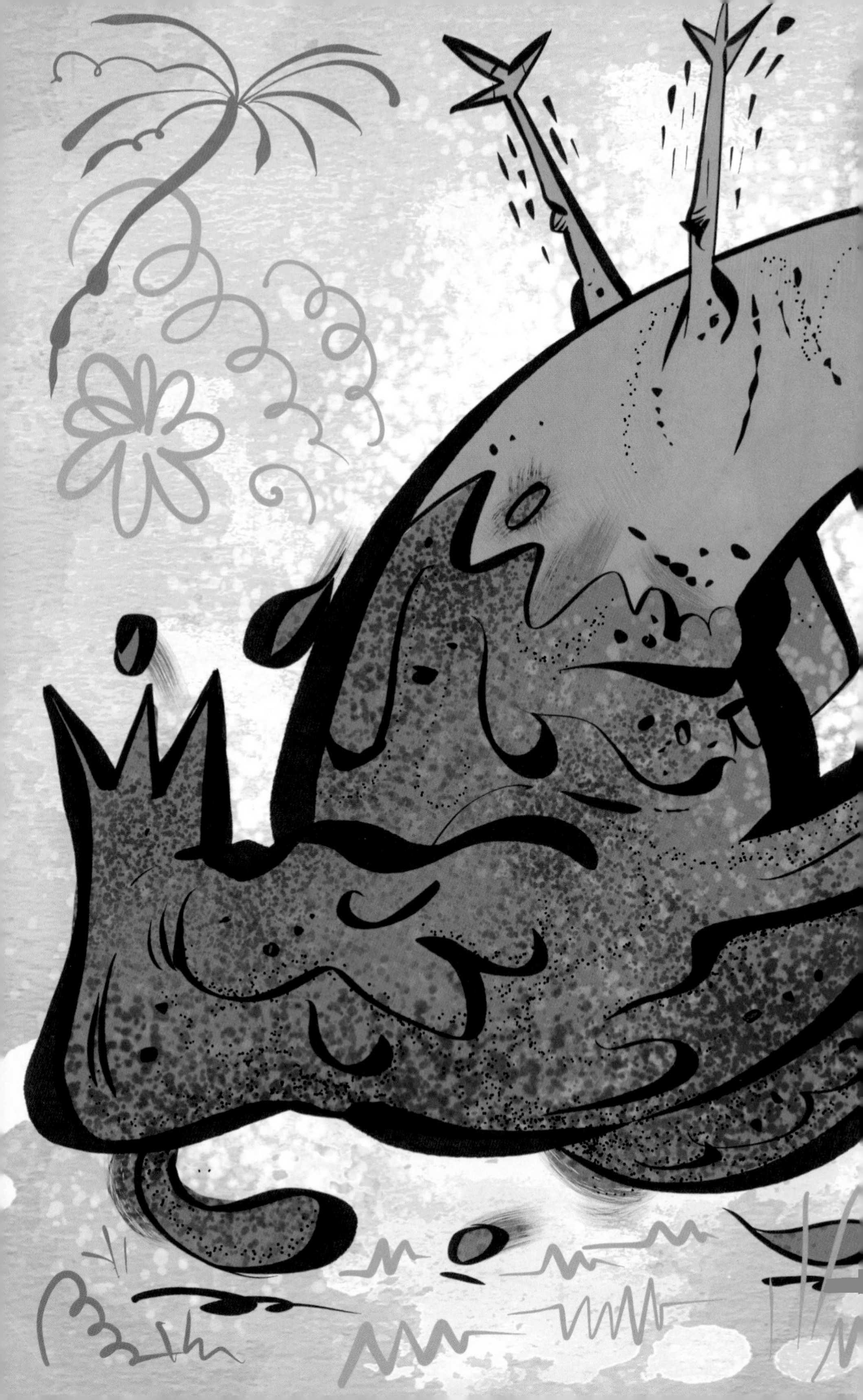

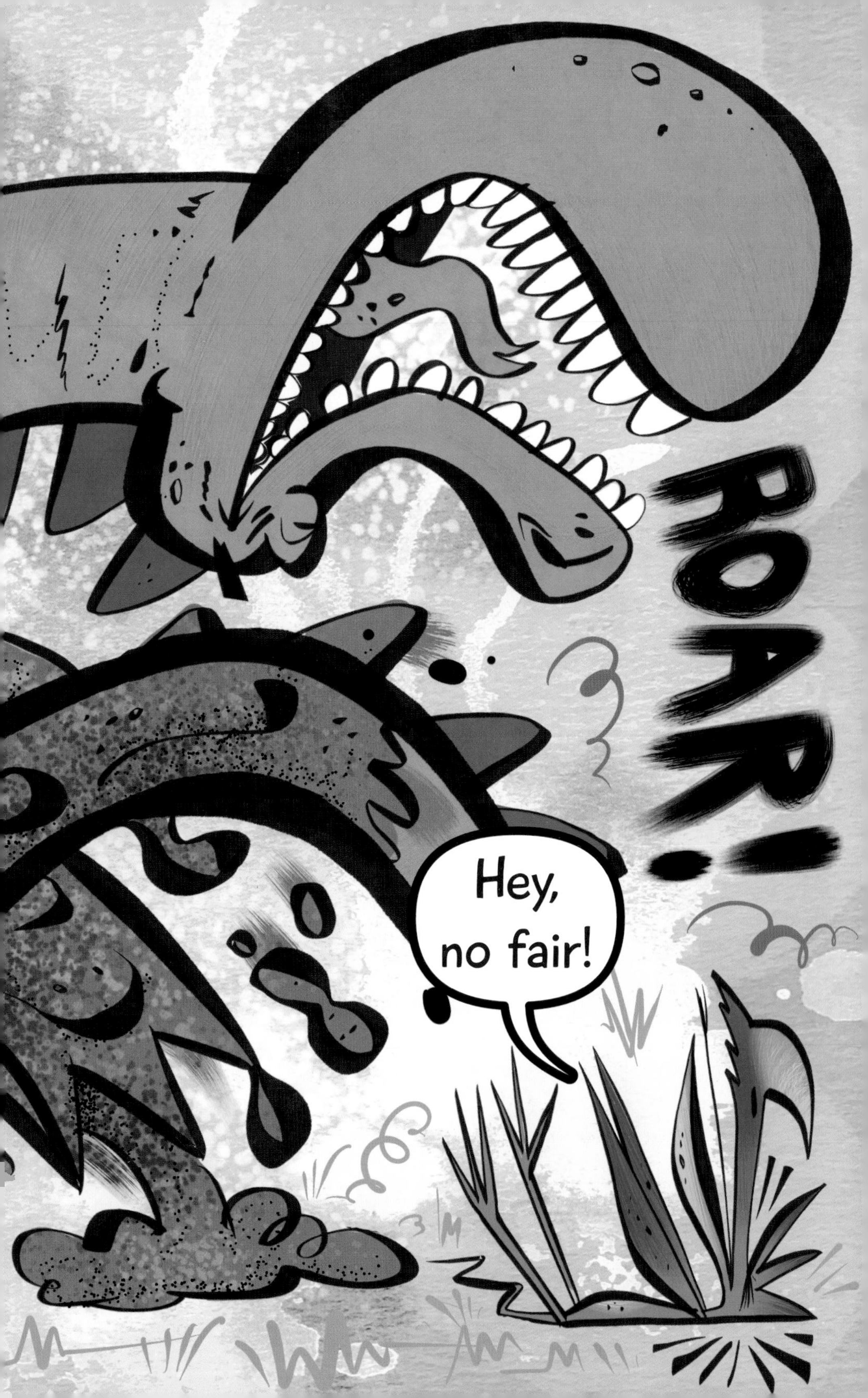
ROAR!!
Hey, no fair!

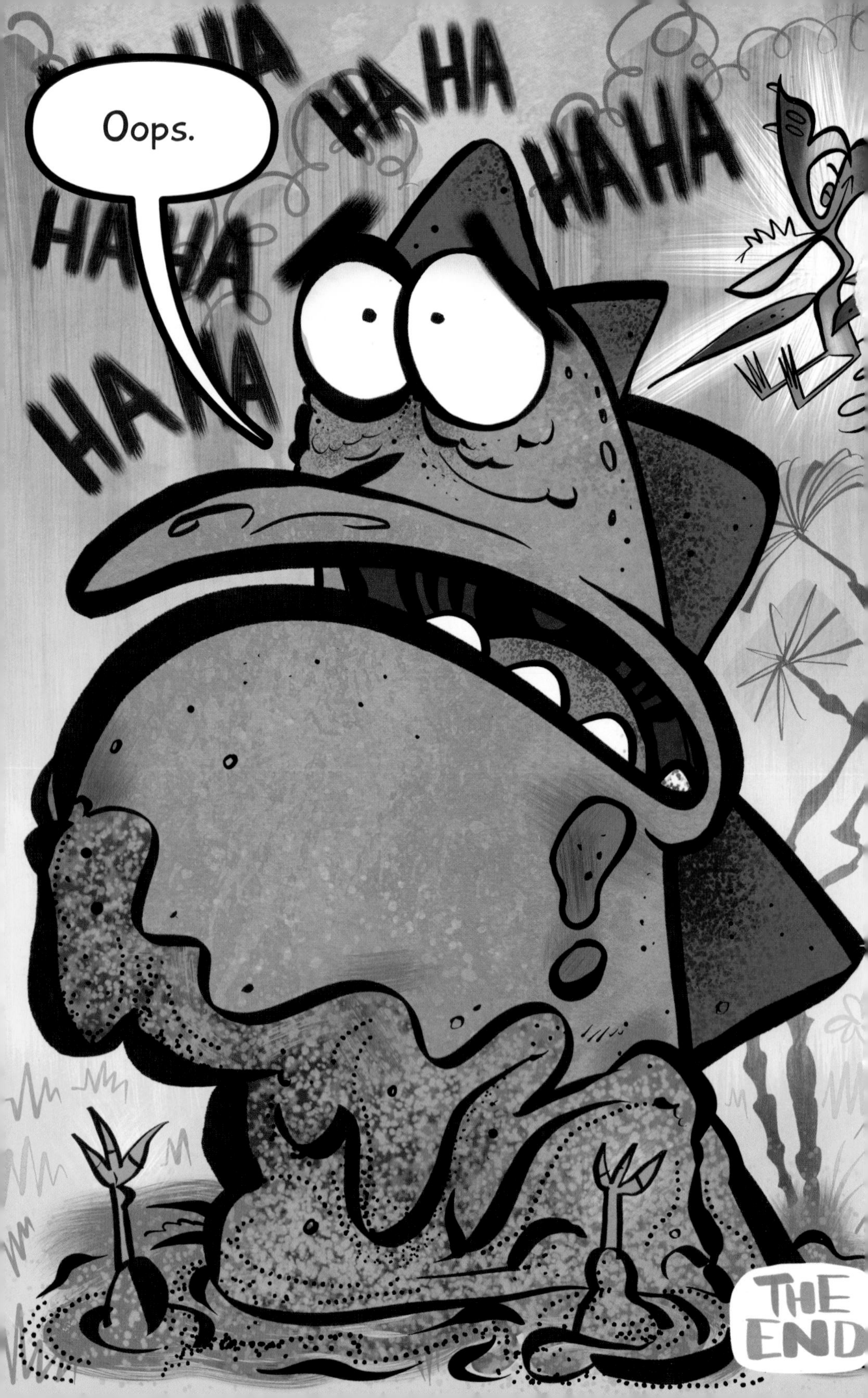
Oops.
HAHA
HAHA
HAHA
HAHA
THE END